ARCANE ALCHEMY

FREYA'S FATE

A HELSDATTER SAGA NOVELLA

RORI BLEU

ROSIE CHAPEL

First printing: 2023
ISBN: 978-0-6459731-6-7 (eBook)
ISBN: 978-0-6459731-7-4 (Paperback)

Ulfire Pty. Ltd.
P.O. Box 1481
South Perth
WA 6951
Australia

Cover Design: R Norman

❀ Created with Vellum

ARCANE ALCHEMY

Freya's Fate

Rori Bleu

Rosie Chapel

PROLOGUE

"**F**reya, you don't have to leave," Sela begged her friend. "There is plenty of room at our place."

'Room' in a New York sense meant Freya could continue to sleep on the couch of Sela and Loki's one-bedroom Manhattan apartment. As tempting as a tenth-floor view of the Park might be to most, another night of trying to block out the lovebirds in the adjacent bedroom was untenable.

Smiling, Freya shook her head and reiterated her plans, "No, sweetheart, I don't want to be — what do they call it here... the third wheel? — anymore. Besides, I hear Europe is idyllic this time of year.

"I want to catch up with friends there, and sponge off them for a while." She dropped a wink, making Sela chuckle as they sipped their overpriced cappuccinos at a boutique coffee shop along Fifth Avenue.

"I need you here as my maid of honor, Freya. The church ladies are campaigning for their former priest to get married in their church... even if he *was* corrupted by me—"

The two could not help but laugh at Sela's snarky comment.

"—they insist on planning it."

"Do you really want to go through the headache of a religious joining? Wouldn't a handfasting be more... fitting? Do you even believe in this God they worship?"

"I know better than to answer that question with you sitting across from me. One wrong word and you'll turn me to dust."

"I would never think of influencing your answer, my dear," Freya replied, with no hint of humor. "Remember, I'm the goddess of Free Thought as much as I am of Free Love."

"Hmm, so always strings attached. With that in mind, let's just say," Sela said, hoping to end the topic of conversation, "I'm leaving it up to Loki. He's known them longer, and you can battle him over it."

Freya patted her friend's hand. A smile returning to her face at the thought of going to war with Loki.

"Are you sure you want to be a widow so soon after getting married?"

Sela was about to defend her fiancé's capabilities when Freya cut her off. Looking at her watch, the goddess said, "I should be going. My fight leaves in a few hours."

"Y-you're actually flying? What in Odin's name for?"

"I have a ton of frequent flier miles."

"Really? Which airline? I wouldn't mind coming along."

"PussyCat Airlines... and there's only room for one passenger on this flight. Besides, I doubt you'd find the in-flight service desirable. All those furballs fill up the carriage more quickly than you'd think."

Sela knew what Freya meant. The goddess intended to use her cat driven chariot to get there. Why Freya used such

an odd sort of propulsion, Sela could never understand —
although she was not a fan of metal tubes hurtling through
the sky, either — but accepted it as another of her friend's
eccentricities.

Freya stood, preparing to leave. Sela took a last sip of
her coffee, set down the cup, looked up at Freya, and
frowned.

At the back of her mind, Sela knew there was more
behind Freya's decision but all she could think to say was,
"You better stay in touch, and don't let me see on TV that
you were arrested for committing some grand heist. I want
a better reason to visit Europe than to bail you out of a
dismal dungeon."

As if I could stop you from doing anything, Sela thought,
loudly enough for her friend to hear.

"Don't worry, Sela. I'll behave."

"Make sure you do, and bring me home an expensive
wedding gift."

"Will the city of Rome suffice?"

Bending, Freya pressed a kiss to Sela's forehead, and
was gone with a gust of wind.

ONE

F reya was glad of the large floppy hat she had been *persuaded* to purchase by one of the street vendors in Athens. The walk... or rather hike... up to the highest level of the ancient theater was no mean feat under the blazing Greek sun.

Yes, she could have ascended in far less exhausting a manner, but her stubborn need to behave like these mortals had yet to abate. Besides, she had come to appreciate the utter normality of being a tourist.

Puffing from exertion, she paused to catch her breath, then turned and immediately lost it again.

Below, spread out in all its glory... Delphi.

Slack-jawed, Freya sank onto the warm lichen-covered stone, and removed her hat to fan her hot face. "Never did I imagine..." she muttered. Throughout the eons of her existence, of all the incredible places she had been privileged to see, this panorama beat them all.

The graceful semi-circle of the theater, nestled on the southwestern slope of Mount Parnassus, acted as a frame for the site, flowing down towards the Pleistos River in the valley below.

Behind her, the weathered mountainside rose sheer and rugged, to kiss the cloudless azure sky.

In front, the craggy rock was alleviated here and there by hardy bushes, disappearing into the verdant swathes of fir and walnut, and the silvery sage, sea of olives blanketing the lower slopes.

Arriving early, Freya had explored much of the site, from the Roman Agora, through the treasuries, and past the Sybil rock on her way to the Temple of Apollo before climbing to the top of the theater. While she appreciated the archaeological importance of the ruins, ancient history was nothing new to her, being older than most of it.

The appeal to Freya was the sense of harmony with the earth... with nature... that the site engendered, and the tranquility — despite the number of visitors — was a balm to her bruised soul.

She could stay here forever.

Leaning back against the remains of what was once a marble seat, she let her mind roam.

When she left New York, Freya had no specific destination in mind, and left the decision to her cats, who chose Istanbul — for no reason Freya could decipher, although the fact it was the capital of Turkey may have been their inspiration.

Her, "you do realize Turkey does not mean the place of the edible fowl," was met with the feline equivalent of a disgusted eyeroll.

Never mind, they were there, and Freya was determined not to let a single day go to waste.

A bustling metropolis, the city was a cacophony of sights, sounds, colors, and smells... some good, some best forgotten. Freya preferred the back streets and the path less trodden, deliberately avoiding the typical tourist haunts; she wanted to experience the true Istanbul, not its façade.

She did, however, venture into the Hagia Sophia, not only lured by tales of its magnificence — which, to be fair, were quite true — but also in search of two inscriptions tucked away in the southern gallery. She had learned about them on a documentary Sela made her watch and, since she was here, why not?

Following a trail of tourists, she was rewarded with a little runic graffiti, etched into the marble by a certain Halfdan and, further around, another by his compatriot, Arí. Possibly members of the Varangian Guard — the emperor's protection detail — and, although mostly illegible, the carvings implied that even Viking warriors get bored.

"They were probably tired of listening to some pompous barbarian, drone on about their magnificence. Been there, heard that." Freya chuckled, to vexed, "Shush"-es from those nearby.

"Hmmm, maybe they were part of a plundering force, and left this as a warning... *Don't mess with Halfdan, he knows where you live.* Good place for gods to perch mind you." She grinned unrepentantly at the group surrounding her. "Great view."

Amused by her own wit, Freya waved nonchalantly at the frowning killjoys and descended into the sunlight.

The exchange, while insignificant in the scheme of things, left Freya feeling out of sorts and disinclined to loiter in what had been the capital of the Eastern Roman Empire until 1453. She was a goddess, she didn't need to be ticked off by ignorant nobodies.

Grumpily, she summoned her chariot and suggested to her cats that they might like to transport her to a place where Gods were revered.

Which is how she ended up at Delphi.

Athens proved to be as chaotic as Istanbul and, after the obligatory tour of the Acropolis, outwardly agreeing with the voluble guide that it was a travesty the British museum had not yet returned the marbles, while inwardly perplexed as to why they cared so much about a child's game, Freya fled.

Her spirit needed reviving, not crushing, and she yearned for serenity. Somewhere to heal, and to adjust. To be restored. To reconnect with the ancients... if they lingered.

The receptionist at the hotel had suggested she do some island hopping, take in the beaches and swim in the warm waters of the Mediterranean. She had even pulled up pictures of Mykonos, Paros, and Naxos on the clever machine called a computer — a technology Freya thought more insidious than the entire Norse pantheon put together.

"Thank you, they do look inviting, but I'm not a fan of the beach, my skin you know..." Freya waved at her porcelain complexion, relieved when she saw the knowing nod of the receptionist.

"Ahhh, you must preserve such fine skin. A hat, a hat, you must buy a hat. It is essential. Yiannis, around the

corner... the stall... he sells many hats. Best price. Go, go..."
The woman had beamed, all but shooing Freya into the
street, her gentle Ionian accent making her instructions
sound like poetry.

Unwilling to upset the genial clerk, and feeling more
like a pickled vegetable than a goddess, Freya did as she
was bidden. The young, and Adonis-like stallholder
charmed his new customer into the behemoth of a hat she
now sported, with barely a flash of his white teeth.

That he charmed into other things too was neither here
nor there... well, she was on holiday.

Aren't romances par for the course?

From her hours in front of Sela's television, Freya had
gleaned that illicit affairs with bronzed heart-throbs were
part and parcel of a Mediterranean holiday. It would be an
utter travesty to flout tradition.

While the nights of torrid lovemaking with the
delectable Yiannis made Freya feel cherished and desired,
they were not enough to dispel the disquiet kindled by her
days searching ancient ruins.

An ardent Greek, Yiannis had waxed lyrical about his
country, in particular — because he had grown up nearby
— the archaeological site at Delphi and associated
wonders.

His enthusiasm had given Freya the excuse to leave
without hurting her lover's feelings and, after assuring him
of her return, left him in a state of goddess-induced bliss.

Freya huffed a disconsolate sigh.

Overhearing snippets of conversation implied that
although mortals were fascinated by the ruins and

intrigued by the reasons they were erected originally, gods and goddesses were nothing more than myth. A way to explain or apportion blame to things they could not understand.

"I am so sorry, Zeus," Freya whispered to the wind. "You and your fellow Olympians did not deserve to be treated with so little respect. Perhaps one day they will recall your worth."

She was almost certain she heard a melancholy lament... or was it naught but a zephyr soughing through the fissures in the stones?

Shaking her head — dwelling on what had been lost was not getting her anywhere — Freya stood, and stretched, enjoying the afternoon breeze on her face.

Yes, she could stay here forever, but the day was waning. She had to get back to the modern town, which shared the same name as the oracle, and where she was staying. It was not far, and she did not actually need to walk, but materializing in the middle of a hotel might raise the odd eyebrow.

"Perfection, thy name is Delphi," she murmured. Patting the ancient stone in tacit farewell, she rammed the hat on her head, and taking care not to twist her ankle, set off down the hill.

TWO

Opting *not* to return to Athens and the welcoming arms of the impossibly handsome Yiannis, Freya pointed her chariot west.

Her goal, the Italian peninsula.

Roman deities were younger than those of Greece. From Sela's obsession with history documentaries, Freya had gleaned that Italy in general and Rome in particular offered an abundance of temples to their vast array of deities.

This gave her a flicker of hope. Had the populace retained their reverence, or had they too consigned their gods to booklets and information markers?

There was only one way to find out.

Regrettably, her optimism was dashed, almost before it had chance to flourish.

Freya traveled the length and breadth of Italy. She was pleased to note the various sites were frequented by more than mobs of vacuous tourists who simply wanted to tick it off their list of must-sees.

Archaeologists, academics, and armchair historians swarmed around the ruins, lauding the Romans, from their ingenuity to their culture, from their engineering skills to their art and architecture, from their business and economic acumen to their military prowess.

Freya could not deny the impact the Romans had in antiquity and in the modern world of the mortals, but it was secular not spiritual. Yes, once upon a time, the people petitioned their gods, but that was no longer the norm... or, had their focus shifted?

She *was* taken aback by the number of churches which littered the capital. The faith practiced by the followers of this Jesus Christ, a humble carpenter who lived in the early first century AD, seemed to have supplanted every other ideology to become the overarching religion.

This gave Freya pause. "Do mortals identify with the man *because* he was..." it galled her to say it... "*ordinary*? Yet they also call him the Son of God. Which God?" she asked herself.

Is it the same across the world? It seemed plausible. *Had not Loki chosen to hide himself in it?*

Certainly, he was no son of Odin or, as far as she could discern, related to any of the Greek, Roman, or Egyptian pantheons.

She had a vague understanding of Christianity... who among her peers didn't?

Loki's stint as a Catholic priest had afforded her a deeper insight.

Just because they were Norse gods and as old as time itself, did not mean they were oblivious to the fluctuations in the ideologies adopted by mortals.

Until now, she had not given it much credence.

"Why do people believe in this man?" She sought an answer from a monk-like cleric in one of the more opulent churches — endlessly amazed she had not been struck by lightning for daring to set foot in a so-called house of God.

She had listened to him talking to a group of tourists about the church, and deemed him to be of higher-than-average intellect; a person with whom she could discuss the esoteric. That he spoke English, albeit with a strong Irish lilt was a fortuitous bonus, and reminded her of Loki's alter ego, Father Thomas.

When Loki told her the world seemed to expect the priests of this religion to have a Hibernian dialect, was he actually being serious for once in his life?

Freya's pretty nose crinkled in thought, *an odd requirement... although his words* do *soothe.*

She followed the black-robed cleric to the cloister garden at the side of the basilica and, leaning against a slender, spiraled pillar, posed her conundrum.

"I think it is because people relate to a human with human failings, more than they do the perfect gods and goddesses of say Greece or Egypt. We can emulate the life of a man who was humble, who was flawed, but who strove to overcome," he said.

"Yet you call him the Son of God. How do you equate the two?"

The cleric raised a suspicious brow at the glamorous, blonde woman with the Scandinavian accent who was giving him the third-degree about the tenets of his faith.

Her perplexed expression suggested genuine interest rather than an attempt to outsmart him.

He escorted her to one of the creaky wooden benches

tucked around the quadrangle, introducing himself as, "Father Dominic."

"I am Freya," she said without thinking, then cursed under her breath at her lapse.

Father Dominic's only reaction, to Freya's relief, was to say, "An ancient name."

Steepling his fingers together, he corralled his thoughts.

The woman's question was not unusual - it was asked in one form or another almost every day. No, it was the vaguely unsettling impression, his answer would have far-reaching consequences.

He shook off the notion, took a breath, and prayed for divine intervention should this get out of hand.

"Okay, without over complicating matters, we believe that God and Christ are one and the same, that Jesus Christ was 'born' of a virgin... therefore purity begat by purity... and was, for want of a better word, 'sent' to save humanity from their sins, fulfilling prophecies laid down in the Old Testament.

"By his death and subsequent resurrection, he defeated Satan... or evil... whatever you choose to call it... and paid the ultimate price for the aforementioned sins."

"So, he *is* immortal?" A concept with which Freya could identify.

"In a manner of speaking, but only briefly. Our faith holds that he ascended to heaven forty days after his resurrection.

She frowned. "Where is he now? For it is not Valhalla or Fólkvangr."

Once again, she had spoken without thinking, but Father Dominic did not seem to register her reference to the halls of the slain. Unbeknownst to Freya, allusions to the people and places attributed to myth and legend were not wholly uncommon.

"Each religion has its own version, or perception of heaven. Perhaps most easily understood as a transcendental paradise where deities, angels, venerable souls and, of course, the faithful go when they die."

"Oh, like Valinor in that book about the ring?" she countered, her face the picture of innocence.

The cleric pinched the bridge of his nose. *This was going to get messy.*

Freya took pity on him.

"Forgive me, I do not wish to get caught up in a deep theological debate. I want to understand why ancient gods and goddesses are no longer revered.

"What changed so drastically that a simple mortal reduces the most powerful beings in the universe to a statue in a ruin?"

"Because powerful beings have no checks and balances. They are limitless, immeasurable, and inexhaustible, which inevitably leads to strife and a battle for supremacy."

"Yet, and I repeat, you believe in one god."

"Yes, *one* God. There are no other Gods to usurp him, or... if you believe the books and the movies... squabble over power like whiny brats arguing over a toy.

"There is just him."

"Or her," Freya interjected with a sly smile.

"Or her," Father Dominic conceded with a dip of his head. "Although an ongoing discussion, faith is faith. It is intangible, ephemeral, and often indescribable.

"Why does this bother you? What are you seeking?"

Staring out over the neatly tended garden, Freya was quiet for so long, Father Dominic wondered whether she had actually heard him, and was about to repeat his question when she spoke.

"My own peace. I come from a..." she paused, searching for a twenty-first century term to describe the Norse pantheon, "...dysfunctional family. Squabbles are the least of it. I read a story once, in which a character was dying and the only thing to save her was belief. A notion not without merit."

Freya smiled sadly. "Thank you for your time. Your faith intrigues me and I think I understand its attraction, but because of it, I fear my... kin will fade away like those of antiquity, from this realm at least.

"Whether that is good or bad, remains to be seen. It is a shame they cannot be revived by a heartfelt chant."

She patted his gnarled hand and stood. "Good day to you, Father."

With that she was gone, in a flurry of blue silk and a tantalizing hint of an intoxicating perfume, leaving a slack-jawed cleric in her wake.

This realm?

That evening, Freya walked along the Tiber. The river, older than the city it snaked through, gleamed like an expensive claret under a sky, tinged pink by the setting sun. She found the cadence of the water, the shadow-play through the trees on the pathway high above her, and the ever-changing reflections soothing.

Climbing the steps to the Ponte Sant'Angelo, she was startled to see a fast-approaching cloud. She glanced around, but no one seemed perturbed.

The balmy air was filled with the trill of birdsong and

the flapping of wings. From every direction flocks of starlings, hundreds... no, thousands of birds converged above her.

Everyone came to a standstill, as though, right at that moment, the world was holding its breath.

The dance began.

Fluid patterns ebbed and flowed, weaving and whirling, forming, and fading as the birds moved through the sky. Now dense, now diaphanous. It was utterly mesmerizing.

Enchanted by the phenomenon, Freya was, uncharacteristically, lost for words. Nature, once again, providing the solace she needed.

She watched the dazzling display until the last bird had fluttered away. She heard the 'oohs, and ahhs' of the crowd, and the frantic clicking of their cameras.

"How can you be hypnotized by a murmuration, yet forsake the gods as though magic does not exist?"

Freya shook her head.

There was nothing for her here.

THREE

D isillusioned, Freya traipsed across Europe like a wraith, barely staying anywhere long enough to find somewhere to grab a night's sleep, never mind the answer to a question she had almost forgotten she once asked.

Weeks passed with little comfort. Heartsore and uncaring where she ended up — as long as it was *not* New York City — the goddess left all destinations in the paws of her cats.

Nothing seemed to assuage her restlessness. Nothing seemed to inspire or inflame her passion for anything.

Even sex became pedestrian... and she experimented with that *a lot.*

Until she found herself in Dublin.

"What on earth possessed you to choose this backwater?" she scolded her cats when her chariot slewed to a halt in a grove of trees.

They pinned her with identical amber glares, turned their backs, and vanished.

"Why thank you, kindly, my dearest ones. Perhaps

consider a five-star hotel next time," she sniped to the empty air and, with an aggrieved humph, surveyed her surroundings.

Pushing her way out of the thicket, Freya was held motionless by the view which met her eyes.

Rolling out in front of her, acres of lush grass, bordered by trees, all bathed in the golden light of the waning afternoon.

What was this place?

She pivoted slowly, half-expecting to see a huge palace or, at the very least, a castle behind her.

The only structure visible from her vantage point was a tall cross at the far side of the green expanse.

To her right, a herd of deer stared at her, their quizzical expressions drawing a chuckle. "Sorry to disturb you," and, for no logical reason, dipped her head. The sight of the animals evoked long suppressed memories; peaceful days watching reindeer foraging in the Northlands when life was less complicated.

Were they even her memories, or had she absorbed them from Sela?

Right at that moment she did not care; their presence was comforting.

She took a deep breath; the air was soft, prompting her to inhale another lungful, then a third. Inexplicably, her spirit began to lift.

"Okay, so you're forgiven," she murmured to her fickle feline travel guides. Clearly, they knew what their mistress needed better than she.

"A place to stay might have helped though," she felt moved to add. No sense in pandering to their already lofty egos.

She stood for a while, trying to decide which way to

head. The hum of traffic from beyond the line of trees suggested a road.

As good a place as any to start.

As she struck out, a capacious handbag materialized in her grasp. Shrugging the strap over her shoulder, Freya smiled.

Was this where the answer lay?

Only one way to find out.

Following her nose, a useful trait if one wanted to find somewhere, Freya set a brisk pace and, as luck would have it, before her legs started to protest at this unexpected exercise, she flagged down a passing taxi, with all the aplomb of a seasoned traveler. That she may have *persuaded* the driver her need was more urgent than his actual fare, mattered not.

With a gentle *nudge*, Freya directed the vehicle to the grandest hotel in the city's center. Shortly thereafter, she alighted outside a regal building on Westmoreland Street.

Thanking her driver, she tipped him generously, hearing his radio crackle to life as she closed the door.

Imagining the conversation between dispatcher and driver, Freya chuckled to herself, as she stepped through the glass doors into a foyer which stopped her in her tracks.

Old world charm blended effortlessly with elegant sophistication, evidenced in the antique sofas and chairs, hugging the edge of the marble-tiled floor, and the light pouring through the glass ceiling which seemed to float high above her.

Eying the three, smartly dressed clerks behind their

respective, highly polished, aged oak desks, at the far side, she approached the one she deemed the easiest to inveigle.

The young man all but fell over himself to assure the breathtakingly beautiful woman in front of him, she did not need a reservation.

"Absolutely, ma'am, we have plenty of rooms available. We are between seasons," he felt it necessary to clarify.

"Excellent. I have heard such wonderful things about your hotel from a dear friend, who recommended I request a quiet suite, if that is at all possible..." she leaned a little closer, ensuring her *assets* did not go unnoticed, and purred, "...James."

By this stage, James could no more deny this guest whatever she asked for, than he could fly to the moon. "I am sure we can offer you the best." He dipped his head, fighting the urge to bow with a medieval flourish; the strangest notion this woman was nobility pestering the periphery of his consciousness.

"You are too kind," Freya dazzled him with a radiant smile, and he nearly swore lifelong fealty there and then. Gathering his wits, he completed the registration process, committing Hilde Lothbrok along with her fictitious address and fake passport details to their system.

Mildly perplexed at Ms. Lothbrok's lack of luggage, James escorted Freya to the simply titled, Trinity Suite.

"This is our most prized suite. Very quiet, but offers stunning views, and all the space a person on holiday might need." James showed her the numerous amenities.

This had to be the greatest understatement Freya had ever heard. The 'suite' was bigger than Sela and Loki's apartment... and, quite possibly, the entire storey it sat on.

Split-level, the upper floor sported a king-sized bed,

dressing room, a bathroom — complete with a spa bath, rainfall shower, and a Nordic steam room. This last intrigued Freya and she made a mental note to investigate as soon as she was alone.

The main area consisted of a well-apportioned lounge, and adjacent dining room to which was attached a kind of butler's pantry where the ever-helpful James pointed out the tea and coffee making facilities, the fridge, sink, crockery and cutlery, and washer/dryer.

The highlight of the suite, in James' opinion, was the rooftop terrace, accessed by a wrought-iron, spiral staircase, overlooking the Trinity College precinct. Under a small, vine entwined pergola — which offered protection from the unpredictable weather — a wicker sofa and two chairs circled a low table.

"Wonderful place to sit with a glass of something and watch the sunset," he said. "'Tis a cracking city, so it is." He gave into his earlier impulse and bowed.

"James, your chivalry warms my heart. A quality missing from so many these days." Freya heaved a forlorn sigh. "I think you and I are going to become good friends." She smiled sweetly, and squeezed his hand, making James her slave forever.

"Anything you want, anything at all, just ring reception." He bowed again, gave her the keycard, and backed out of the room, leaving Freya in peace.

A decent meal in the hotel's restaurant, and a better night's sleep than she had managed for longer than she could remember, Freya felt almost... well... human.

Consulting with a different and very obliging receptionist by the name of Maeve, Freya — armed with leaflets and maps, her ears ringing with the best places to start — set out to explore Dublin.

As she strolled along the wide, tree-lined, and sunlit streets, Freya registered a frisson of happiness, the first for eons. A good sign, and one she took to mean her cats had chosen this quaint city for more than just its charm.

Sela had introduced her to coffee — an ambrosial beverage of which she believed she was becoming quite the aficionado. The day was warm for September and, passing a café with outside seating, Freya decided to fortify herself with a large mug of it before immersing herself in the delights Dublin had to offer.

Sipping what the menu described as an Americano and nibbling a sweet pastry, Freya poured over the map, checking the sites Maeve had circled against the corresponding leaflet.

She definitely wanted to see this Book of Kells. Maeve had assured her it was worth the entry fee and she could include a tour of the college while she was there.

Not far beyond Trinity College was the site which had piqued Freya's interest more than any other when the kindly receptionist had been going through the numerous things to see. The permanent Viking Exhibition at the National Museum of Ireland. Apparently, in the same building, there was also a Treasury and an Egyptian exhibition.

All three, an absolute must as far as Freya was concerned.

"Is everything ok?" A voice to her left asked.

Freya glanced up to see the waitress hovering. "Thank you, as delicious as promised." She smiled. "I intend to return to try one of those chocolate cakes."

"Oh, that's grand." The young girl beamed her appreciation. "I look forward te seein' yer soon then."

"Count on it." Freya was proud of her recently acquired collection of colloquialisms. Draining her coffee, she gathered her stuff into a neat pile and headed for Kildare Street and the museum.

FOUR

E ven before she had set foot in the museum, Freya
was held speechless by the grandeur of its soft gray
and cream façade, reminiscent of the ancient
buildings she had explored on her Grand Tour.

In the center of what she later discovered was described
as a Palladian-style building, and suspended above the
colonnaded entryway, a domed glass rotunda.

The exterior called to mind the Pantheon in Rome, a
monument Freya had connected with more than she had
anticipated. An impression enhanced by the glorious interior, with its mosaic floors, slender marble columns, intricate wrought iron scroll-work, and classical motifs.

Stunned that this jaw-dropping place did not charge
visitors to view the delights within, Freya, although
desperate to see the Viking exhibit, opted to tour the
displays in chronological order. She had nothing else to do
and nowhere else to be... *why rush*?

Two hours later, Freya stepped into the sunshine, her
mind spinning with everything she had seen.

An incredible collection of artifacts spanning almost ten

millennia. From Ancient Egypt, through the Stone, Bronze, and Iron Ages, to classical antiquity. From the end of the Roman empire, through the Viking era, right up to the current century.

What was the phrase beloved of teenagers...? Mind blowing.

While not incognizant of the history of the world, Freya had not *seen* much of it, and was astonished by what had survived the ravages of time, and the mishandling of mortals.

Her stomach rumbled, reminding her it was well past lunchtime. Unaware of where the best eateries were, she just walked until she spotted somewhere that looked inviting.

Coming to a corner, she paused, trying to decide which way to go.

"Are ye lost?" The question was asked in a rich lilting brogue.

"Not lost as much as trying not to be found," Freya replied cryptically, pivoting on her heel to pin the speaker with a 'don't mess with me' look.

The man, *and oh my goodness this was the very definition of a man*, in front of her, smiled engagingly. His chestnut hair, deep green eyes and neatly trimmed beard attesting to his Viking ancestry and, to Freya, an irresistible combination. That he was tall, and drop-dead gorgeous merely an added bonus.

"Can I help ye find yer way, then?" he pressed.

"I am in search of a suitable eating establishment," she said primly.

"Well, seems the Gods are smilin' on yer. I know the perfect place." He dipped his head. "Sean Kavanagh, at yer service."

For reasons he could not fathom, Sean crooked his arm,

gratified, after a slight hesitation on the stranger's part, to feel her fingers slide around his sleeve.

"I am Freya," she provided her real name without thinking, then held her breath ready to wield a little magic if necessary.

It was not.

"Oh, that's lovely, so 'tis. One o' me friends, lives in Australia now, called his daughter Freya. Nice that the old names are coming back into fashion."

Freya relaxed and listened to him prattling on about names and traditions as he escorted her along a side street coming to a halt outside an old stone building.

Above the door, a shiny black oblong bore the name *The Oak Tree* in gilt letters, and one of the knots Freya was becoming familiar with. Several small squares with various logos flanked the open door; closer inspection of which seemed either to back up Sean's assertion, or apprised the customer of the different forms of payment accepted within.

"Here yer go, best food in Dublin," Sean nodded at the building.

Freya arched a skeptical brow. "A sweeping statement, if ever I heard one."

"I promise yer." He twinkled.

That did it.

"Fine, Mr. Sean Kavanagh, I shall hold you to your word." Freya allowed herself to be ushered inside. She paused on the threshold, caught off guard by the inviting ambience of the tavern.

Through open archways, either side of where she stood, Freya could see two more rooms. Signs above each arch indicated the room on the right to be *The Snug,* and the left to be *The Nook* — the latter set up like a formal dining area.

The dark wood of the tables, chairs, and bar area was complemented by the green, bronze, and gold of the soft furnishings.

A fire crackled merrily in the stone hearth, which Freya imagined would make her feel overheated, but the temperature in the room was just right.

The same knot from the sign was etched into the windows, painted on the panels of the bar, printed on the coasters and the menus, and woven into the carpet.

"Come on in and take a load off."

Sean was hailed by one or two people as he led her across to the bar where he pulled out a stool, and gestured for her to take a seat.

Unused to perching on so high a chair, Freya — hand on the bar for leverage — hoisted herself onto it with a modicum of grace.

Shuffling until comfortable, she glanced around, saying 'Hello' when Sean introduced her to one or two of the customers who were within earshot.

"On holiday?" one asked, nursing a glass of dense, dark brown, almost black liquid, topped with a layer of creamy foam.

"Something like that," Freya hedged.

"Tryin' not to be found," Sean interjected.

"Ah, no better place to lose yourself in, than Dublin, lovey." The customer belched softly, to murmurs of agreement from several clientele.

"This is only my first day, but I am enthralled," Freya smiled. Clearly, the correct answer, given the muffled cheers and sage nods.

"That's it, Miss Freya, you've won their hearts in that one reply." Sean chuckled. "Have you sampled our famous brew yet?"

"Coffee?" Freya essayed, hopefully.

"Coffee? Pah. No, Guinness. Drink of the Gods."

This is the second time he has mentioned the Gods. Perhaps Ireland is indeed their sanctuary. Maybe this was not a complete waste of time and energy, Freya mused thoughtfully, saying out loud, "No, I have not heard of this beverage."

Her words fell into an unexpected silence and all eyes swiveled to her.

Freya stared, astonished by their reaction. "What? What did I do?"

"Yer've not heard of Guinness? You been living under a rock?" A wiry-looking gentleman with a shock of white hair, sitting in the corner, quizzed. "Geez, the world is going to hell in a handbasket."

A bark of laughter prompted Freya to glance over her shoulder.

Sean was tying a black apron around his waist. Light dawned.

This *was why he said The Oak Tree served the best food. He damn well works here.*

Her deadpan blue gaze was met with one of innocent green; her head shake earned a wry chuckle.

"Leave her be, Liam. Yer'll scare her away, and she hasn't tasted me stew yet."

Freya watched Sean pull one of the knobs on the bar, slowly, the black handle bore the image of a golden harp.

He repeated his action twice, then lifted a glass full of the same dark liquid, the patron who first addressed her was drinking. In fact, as she scanned the bar, she registered most were supping the same ale.

"Pay them no mind. What they lack in tact they make up for in tips. Get your smackers around that." Sean advised.

Not entirely certain what 'smackers' were, Freya, conscious everyone was watching, took a judicious sniff. To her relief, it smelt palatable and, as yet none of the patrons had keeled over.

Closing her eyes, she sipped the rich ale which flowed through the creamy foam.

Freya did not think anything could beat coffee, but this Guinness was surely a potion brewed by the Gods. The malty sweetness was countered by the bitter flavor of hops, and she swore there were hints of chocolate and coffee.

Absolute nectar!

Putting the glass on the counter, she studied the sea of avid faces surrounding her.

"I do believe that is the most delectable ale I have ever drunk." She dimpled at the crowd, wholly unaware the foam had left a moustache on her upper lip.

The silence was broken by guffaws and a general slapping of backs.

"You can add undying devotion to the list." Sean grinned, as he slid a steaming bowl of food across the polished surface of the bar. "Irish Stew, compliments of the chef."

"Oh, I cannot leave you without coin," Freya protested.

Putting Freya's odd turn of phrase to the nuances of language, Sean waved off her qualms. "Irish hospitality. Eat."

The aroma of the food was making Freya's stomach growl. Blushing, she picked up her fork and devoured the meal, conceding as she scraped every last morsel from the bowl, Sean's claim was not erroneous.

"That was sublime." She smiled a trifle embarrassed by her appetite. "Mind, I may never eat again."

"Always trust the word of an Irishman." Sean quipped. "Never put yer astray."

"I may have to beg that recipe from you."

"Ahh." He tapped his nose. "Family secret, passed down for generations. Me old granny would turn in her grave if I gave it away."

"Hmmm... fair enough." Freya drained her glass, and requested a second, to the amusement of the other patrons who, now they considered her one of them, tumbled over themselves to pose questions, in the main because they were flummoxed as to why she was all alone in a big city.

She fended them off good-humoredly and, without actually giving them any information at all, had them believing she had shared her innermost secrets.

During a lull in conversation, Freya, who had been fiddling with her beer mat, absently, turned it over in her hands, studying the pattern.

"This knot." Freya traced it with her finger, sensing the innate power of the design.

Did Sean realize its significance?

"What prompted you to choose this motif? The design is not dissimilar to the ancient Ringerike and Urnes art styles."

Not wholly cognizant of what she was referring to, Sean plucked the coaster from her grasp. "'Tis called a Dara Knot, and symbolizes wisdom and strength."

"Dara?"

"Comes from doire, Irish for oak tree."

"Ahhh, I understand." Freya nodded. "I know a thing or two about trees. They are sacred, a way to connect us to the spirit world, and are considered to be doorways to other realms.

"In my... culture, the ash holds special significance." She

did not feel it pertinent to explain the importance of Yggdrasil; these people were strangers.

"The oak is that way for the Irish." Sean said. He pointed to the pattern.

"See, there is no beginning and no end, the intertwined lines represent the prodigious root system, allowing the robust tree to withstand almost anything."

His words struck a chord with Freya.

This must be the reason the cats chose Dublin.

If she was unsure, Sean's next remark, almost as an aside, confirmed her suspicions.

"The oak also represents immortality."

"I-immortality?" Freya stammered, nonplussed.

Was there more to this man than met the eye?

He shrugged. "The oak tends to be one of the tallest trees in the woods and prone to being struck by lightning. It rarely kills the tree, they survive and continue to grow. Immortal."

FIVE

ighting to curb her curiosity elicited by Sean's explanation, Freya tucked it away to be revisited, hopefully, at a later time, covered her inquisitiveness with an aplomb honed over centuries, and changed the subject.

Hours vanished as the animated chatter ebbed and flowed, the taproom ringing with laughter.

One of the patrons asked Freya where she was from. The truth being stranger than fiction, she tried to be as honest as possible.

"Norway, although my family can be traced back to before the lands of Scandinavia were carved up."

"Before the Vikings then?" another piped up.

"Long before." She grinned. "They assimilated quite well here, did they not? At least, compared with other parts of the British Isles. I spent a few hours in the museum today," she added by way of clarification, nodding in its general direction. "The exhibition is most informative. Their influence on your art and architecture is astonishing and enduring."

"Aye, the buggers certainly left their mark. Mind, the invasions served to unite the native folk, a lot o' good it did 'em."

"I understand their tactics were rapid incursion, capture the maximum amount of valuable goods and destroy what was unable to be taken, then flee the vicinity before your ancestors could mount an effective response."

"Pretty much," Sean interjected, resting his elbows on the bar. "With hindsight, we can appreciate the impact the invasions had, but I don't imagine the locals were best chuffed at the time. Warriors like the Vikings had little sympathy for the people they were trying to subjugate."

"The complaint of every conquered nation since time began, I should imagine," Freya said. "My... research suggests they settled relatively quickly though. Places like Angassen and Dublin, later Waterford and Limerick prospered under Viking rule."

"Goodness, you sound like a walking textbook. You certainly paid close attention to the placards," Liam teased.

Freya blushed. "Ok, full disclosure, Norse history is my errr... specialty... you might say. I have been... hmmm... studying it for more years than I care to count, with emphasis on their art.

"The integration and adaptation of the Norse styles by Irish artisans and craftsmen coincides with the fluctuating successes of the Viking raids and a burgeoning, if grudging, relationship between the two cultures.

"Conversely, I love that acceptance was not universal and is still visible in the subtle condemnation found on ancient stone carvings, particularly the High Crosses, as well as the illuminated manuscripts, both remaining obstinately traditional well into the Viking period."

Despite her formal turn of phrase, her remarks had

attracted quite the audience who encouraged her, shamelessly.

Always happy to listen to people talk about their beloved country, none appeared in the slightest fazed that Freya's knowledge seemed to include a wealth of detail which extended beyond that of even the most learned professor.

"Sure, 'tis an expert you are." Sean grinned at her as she sipped her fourth Guinness, secretly impressed by her knowledge, not to mention her ability to hold her alcohol.

"Oh, I don't think so, more like a passionate amateur." Freya demurred.

"As it happens, me own family can be traced back to before the Viking invasions," Sean supplied *that* gem with casual airiness.

"One of the manuscripts in the museum was passed down through the generations, until me great, great..." he counted backwards in his head, "...I think that's enough greats... granddaddy offered it to the curator who, apparently, couldn't believe his luck. Been part of the collection ever since.

"It dates to when Dublin was an ecclesiastical settlement, around the time of the first incursion, and much too valuable an artifact to keep in a desk. If you believe the story, the manuscript was stolen around 1817, at the order of some greedy English earl. A distant cousin 'retrieved' it," Sean air-comma'd the word retrieved, "killing the earl in the process."

"Oh, a murder mystery." Freya stared agog, as she ran her mind back over the Viking exhibit. She recalled being riveted by the manuscript to which he referred, and had read the placard explaining its origins. "Wait, I saw that this morning. That was *yours*? Oh, my goodness, what a treasure. We are fortunate indeed, your ancestor felt able to gift it to the museum."

"Oh, it wasn't a gift, he expected them to pay handsomely for the honor." Sean grimaced. "Pappa Kavanagh was not the altruistic benefactor everyone believed him to be. I reckon he'd have squeezed the last drop of blood from a dying man. Ah well, can't change the past.

"How long did you say you're staying?" He went off on a tangent as an idea struck him.

"I didn't," she countered.

"In my opinion, be it ever so humble, I reckon you should try to get a gig at the museum as a guide. I think they are looking for volunteers especially in the lead up to Christmas. You'd be a hit. Wouldn't even need training."

"A gig?" The word floored Freya.

Sean didn't seem to notice. "You know, a job... well, not really a job because it's unpaid. You escort small groups around the exhibits, sometimes tourists, sometimes school kids, and the like."

The notion appealed to Freya. "You think they might be interested?"

"I think they would be foolish to pass up the opportunity."

"I shall consider it, thank you Sean." She smiled, her blue eyes shining, and it was all Sean could do not to drag her over the bar and kiss her senseless.

Freya glanced at the clock on the wall behind the bar. It was almost six, probably time to think about returning to her accomodation.

Reluctantly, she started to shimmy off the tall stool.

"I suppose I ought to find my way back to the hotel. Thank you for a most entertaining afternoon. I will definitely return for more of that sublime ale."

No one knew quite how she managed it, but as Freya stretched her foot to steady her descent from the stool, she slipped.

Her grace and poise was completely ruined as she gave vent to a muffled screech and let loose a stream of Norse expletives.

Once again, all eyes fell on the exquisite and — had they but known it — goddess, currently hopping about, swearing like a fishwife.

She paused in her antics to glare at the crowd balefully, only to feel her lips twitching at their stunned expressions. The curses transformed into a gale of laughter, which was contagious and the other patrons guffawed uproariously.

Sean came around to check on Freya, who was leaning on the counter wiping tears of mirth from her eyes.

"Let me see that ankle, sure but you cannot be walking if yer've twisted it."

Freya's sparkling blue gaze landed on the handsome bartender and she, innocence personified, lifted her sore foot, relishing the sensation of Sean's gentle fingers examining the joint.

"Perhaps I need another drink while the throbbing subsides." Deeming it unwise to inform them her ankle would be healed before the drink was poured.

"Perhaps yer should stay for dinner and I'll take yer back to yer hotel when me shift finishes."

"When will that be?"

"Eight."

"I do believe you have a deal."

And so, it began.

T rue to his word, Sean took Freya back to her hotel, the latter remembering to favor her right leg to maintain the illusion of a twisted ankle.

Dusk had fallen, the sky morphing from red and cerise through purple to a soft gray, heralding a fine day on the morrow. High above, Venus was clearly visible, her companions flickering into existence. A light breeze rustled through the trees, carrying with it a delicate fragrance.

The city milled with people, but Freya barely noticed, deep in conversation with her handsome escort, unable to prevent herself from preening a little when she spotted the envious glances of passing females.

"Here we are. Home." Sean came to a halt in front of the glass doors. The perfect gentleman, he did not even try to sneak a kiss, although Freya knew it was a hard-fought battle. Chivalry overcame his baser instincts, and he bowed over her hand, making do with a kiss on her palm.

The gesture sent a delicious tingle through the goddess right to her toes.

"I'll be seein' yer soon then." He arched a questioning brow.

"Count on it." She smiled, the lights of the hotel entrance making her blue eyes glisten.

Already halfway in love with the woman, he had met scant hours earlier, it took everything Sean had to walk away.

"Looking forward to it." Sean bowed again and strode off down the path.

Freya watched him leave, admiring his upright bearing and broad shoulders. "Oh, Sean Kavanagh, you are a dangerous, dangerous man."

Emboldened by the enthusiastic encouragement of her new-found friends, Freya, after much soul-searching, approached the museum.

Her knowledge about history in general and Viking history in particular, impressed the lady who organized the volunteers for the winter season. In less time than it takes to spell Scandinavia, the museum had run a security check — the results of which were impeccable, an interesting evaluation for a person with no footprint in Midgard — and Freya was handed a badge, a pass key, and a schedule.

The supervisor assured Freya, she could download the rota onto her phone which paired up with an app specific to the museum.

Baffled by everything about the sentence, Freya brushed it aside with airy insouciance, saying she was too old to be bothered with a phone, which rendered the woman speechless and, by the time she had recovered,

Freya was gone leaving nothing but a faint hint of her perfume.

September slid into October, and Freya's two days a week at the museum became four.

To her badly concealed surprise, the goddess loved it; discovering that imparting knowledge was more rewarding than she anticipated. Even rowdy school kids were transformed into angelic audiences when Freya started to speak.

That she may have *persuaded* them it was in their best interest *not* to behave like savages was neither here nor there and, in truth, benefited everyone.

Her relationship with Sean flourished but, despite their obvious passion for each other, they took it slowly. Inexplicably, Freya wanted to savor the journey instead of skipping straight to the destination.

An unusual state of affairs for the Goddess of Sex and Seduction, but one she relished. Sean was the consummate gentleman, never pushing his own needs, simultaneously driving her to distraction with every kiss. It was utterly delicious.

On their first official date, he admitted *The Oak Tree* had been in his family for generations. Not *quite* as old as The Brazen Head which, he informed Freya, opened in 1198, but had been serving customers for well over hundred and fifty years.

"Must make socializing difficult," Freya had felt a twinge of disappointment when he told her, aware of the long hours involved in managing a bar. *So much for another holiday romance.*

"Aye, but I have good staff, and can afford to take a break now and again. All work and no play makes Sean a very dull boy indeed." He twinkled, wickedly.

Freya's fingers tiptoed down the front of his shirt "Which would not do at all," she purred.

Sean grasped her hand and entwined it with his. "Tease," he chuckled. "Fancy a nightcap?"

Freya frowned, unfamiliar with the word. "Why would I want a night cap? It is not cold."

Sean burst out laughing, only to sober quickly when Freya, suspecting he was making fun of her, disengaged their hands and marched off in a huff.

He caught up with her in three strides and hooked her elbow, spinning her around to face him.

"I'm sorry, *mo chuisle.* I didn't mean t'upset ye. A nightcap is a drink we take afore we go to bed. I assumed everyone knew that. Your English is so good I keep forgetting you're a pesky foreigner." He pulled her close.

Freya didn't understand the Gaelic, but it rolled off Sean's tongue like an endearment. She leaned back in his embrace to glare at him, but his contrite expression and the apology in his alluring green eyes undermined her resolve.

"Forgive me." He kissed her forehead. "Forgive me, *mo mhuirnín.*" He kissed her nose. "Forgive me, *mo chroí.*" he stole her lips with fiery passion.

For once, Sean was relieved Freya had no clue as to the meaning of his words. To profess your... devotion so soon after meeting was presumptuous, but he couldn't help it, and this way it just sounded like nonsense.

Eventually, they came up for air. Freya patted her hair

hoping it didn't look as disheveled as she felt. "Fine, Mr Sean Kavanagh, you are forgiven..."

He started to smile.

"...on the proviso you repeat that with obscene frequency," she held his gaze, "and tell me what those words mean."

Sean's smile blossomed into outright laughter. "Aye, but yer an imp, Miss Freya Lothbrok. Are ye sure yer not related to the fairies?"

"Most definitely not," *Imps? Fairies?* Freya curbed her tongue from running away with itself. *If it wasn't gods, it was fairy folk. Did they believe in them or was it nothing more than a turn of phrase, like a habit?*

She heard Sean promise, "I'll agree to your first demand, as for yer second... one day." with which she had to be satisfied.

She shook her head, time enough for fairies later, *for now...* she stopped thinking about magic and deities, and let Sean weave his own brand of sorcery.

One date led to another and before the blazing autumn leaves began to fall, they were spending every free moment together.

Sean played tour guide, ensuring Freya did not miss out on the best Dublin had to offer. Parks, museums, the zoo, the city, the distilleries, the castle, and everything in between. He took her further afield, exploring the idyllic countryside, with its spectacular coastline.

. . .

One day, while walking one of the shorter trails along Howth Cliff, Sean made a suggestion, which startled Freya so much, she nearly tumbled over the edge.

"What do yer reckon to moving in with me?"

This was the last thing Freya expected to hear, prompting her to take a large and injudicious step sideways. If not for Sean's lightning reflexes, her immortality might have been revealed a whole lot sooner than she wanted... and was prepared for.

"I didna think the idea was so awful, yer'd fling yerself off the cliff to avoid answering me." He tried to make light of it, but Freya registered his confusion at her response.

Moving as far from the edge as the path allowed, Freya gaped at him slack jawed. "I b-beg your pardon, my reaction was one of shock, not abhorrence." Maintaining some semblance of formality as her brain careened with the ramifications of agreeing with his proposal. "Might you say that again?"

Sean repeated his question, adding. "Sure, but it must be costin' yer a fortune stayin' at the hotel. I've got a nice place, yer could even have yer own bedroom if yer prefer... although..." he left that dangling.

A couple almost since they day they met, two months ago, Sean had not taken Freya to his home. This was not for want of invites, Freya was the one determined to keep things at arm's length; a losing battle.

Two months. For Freya, less than the blink of an eye, and they had yet to succumb to the passion their bodies craved. Living together sounded altogether too... permanent an arrangement... *still*... the notion of sharing space with Sean was as tantalizing as it was unnerving.

"How would it work?" the words tripped over her lips before she could prevent them.

Sean smiled broadly, relieved Freya had not dismissed it out of hand. "How about we try a couple of nights, and see how it goes. Nothing's written in stone. If you feel uncomfortable or it's too soon, you still have the hotel."

In truth, Freya had been debating whether to find a small apartment. Not that the cost of the hotel bothered her, but she missed her own space.

Except you won't have your own space, the annoying voice in her head reminded.

"Let me think about it. I have never lived with anyone before," Freya admitted.

Yes, she had shared more beds than she cared to count, including the one of her supposed husband, the reprehensible Asgardian, but she had always retained private living quarters. She had never had any desire to relinquish her autonomy.

Until today.

"So, it's not a no?" Sean interlaced their fingers.

"It's not a no."

By the time they reached the car, Freya, ignoring the warning bells clanging loudly in her head, listened to her heart.

"I suppose a trial couldn't hurt."

Almost before she had finished her sentence, Freya was whisked into Sean's muscular arms and he kissed her into a dizzy spiral.

"Ooof, what was that in aid of. Not that I'm complaining." Freya had to steady herself against his powerful body... not particularly arduous.

"Just sealin' the deal, *mo mhuirnín.*"

"And you still haven't told me what that means."

"One day."

It sounded like they had forever.

SEVEN

Sean's house turned out to be a three-story Georgian townhouse a short distance from *The Oak Tree*. Nestled in a terrace, the warm red brick with cream trim, bay windows, and lofty chimneys seemed to float above a flight of steps which led to an arched, recessed doorway.

"Sean, this is beautiful," Freya breathed when he, rather shyly, helped her out of the car.

"She is pretty special." Sean ushered her up the steps and, after unlocking the door, opened it into the cool, tiled hallway.

"She?" Freya quirked an amused brow.

"All houses are she's," he defended. "Come on, I'll show you around."

The main level sported a large open-plan lounge-dining room, kitchen and what Sean referred to as his den.

"You mean like a man cave? Off limits to the ladies?" Freya quizzed. "Television, mini bar, pool table? Seems pointless when you live alone. Isn't every room your 'man cave?"

"That would be telling." As he took her upstairs, where he pointed out the four bedrooms, one with an ensuite, plus a second bathroom, linen press, and separate toilet.

"This is mine." Sean indicated the room with the ensuite, which also happened to be the largest. Freya was surprised to note it was spotlessly tidy, as had been the rest of the house.

The blue and cream decor complemented by an occasional hint of yellow in the curtains and bedding gave the space an airy feel. Opposite the window, stood a dark wooden-framed king-sized bed, with matching chest of drawers on the adjacent wall. A walk-through closet connected the bedroom to the bathroom where the color palate continued, and was equally neat.

There was a welcoming ambience in this home; it was a haven, a sanctuary. Before she had inspected the basement — fitted out as a laundry, wet room, and extra storage — Freya knew the only reason she would return to the hotel was to collect her luggage.

This is not to say their cohabitation was all wine and roses — although there *was* a lot of wine. Two headstrong personalities trying to navigate the challenges of occupying the same space was never going to be smooth sailing, but both were adult enough to compromise.

At least, Sean was... Freya — being a goddess and used to being pandered to — tended to be a trifle obdurate but, by the time winter held the city in its grip, they had found their rhythm... in more than just their day to day lives.

. . .

True to his word, Sean did not pressure Freya into taking their relationship to the next level, although sharing a house *did* precipitate the inevitable.

They came together with a fiery passion that seemed unslakable, unquenchable. Their need for each other was addictive, stronger than any aphrodisiac, and they craved the high.

Nothing in Freya's long existence prepared her for the ecstasy Sean could induce, seemingly with the barest of touches. She was powerless under his sinful seduction and, for once, had no problem conceding control. Of course, she reciprocated with sensuous interest, bringing Sean to his knees with her uninhibited hedonism.

For a while, it was only their respective jobs which got them out of the bedroom.

It wasn't *just* sex, the pair talked about everything.

Well, almost everything.

Keenly aware that complete honesty would kill their relationship dead in its tracks, Freya was careful not to reveal her true identity, although once or twice her heart nearly overruled her head.

The reason being that the longer she was around these people whose Celtic heritage was steeped in myth and lore, the stronger her conviction that this was the place to revive her wounded soul.

While she could not deny the notion of gods and goddesses lingered around the ancient cities of the Mediterranean, they had faded into memory, consigned to history, and only referred to in that context.

As far as she could tell, here, in Ireland, they were still part of everyday life... creatures like banshees, leprechauns, and fairies were not to be taken lightly.

Similarly, to gods and goddesses, the little people were responsible for all natural, supernatural, and other-worldly phenomena. They could be kind and generous, or angry and vengeful; dispense bad luck as easily as good fortune.

Nobody was ridiculed for their unconditional acceptance of the existence of fairy folk, in fact it was more likely to be the other way around, which fascinated Freya.

One night in the pub, she decided to ask the question.

"What is it about Ireland that perpetuates a belief in the fae?"

Familiar with Freya's propensity to veer into the bizarre, this topic was dear to the hearts of the patrons and all answered at once.

Laughing, she held up her hand. "One at a time, you crazy buggers," dishing out the slang she had adopted with relish.

"I think some of it might be to do with the lack of techy stuff here compared with say Britain." Cormac, Liam's brother, said to nods from the others.

"Some places only got the leccy 'bout forty years ago."

"Electricity," Sean translated at Freya's baffled expression.

"Ahhh, thank you." She beamed at him.

"Anyhoo, suddenly we were catapulted into the twenty-first century, with all the associated industry and technology, skipping all that went on in between," Cormac continued.

"I guess you could say that ancient wisdom and folklore

was never eroded, and now the old sits alongside the new," Tara, one of the barmaids, interjected.

"Do *you* believe?" She looked around the group propping up the bar, these gentle people who had become her friends.

"Of course." To a person they nodded.

"Yet Ireland is staunchly Catholic, does that not jar with the church's teachings?" Freya countered.

"Over the centuries, they've kinda melded together, like an arcane alchemy. Christianity and archaic mythology influenced each other, threads got woven together. Even St. Patrick and St. Brigid are linked to ancient pagan myth." Sean said from behind the polished counter.

"So, in effect, despite modernization, you have not lost your sense of, for want of a better word, magic?" Deliberately, Freya quashed the joy bubbling within, knowing it would manifest as a radiance she could not explain, in spite of their current conversation.

"In a nutshell, yes." Aileen, Liam's wife, whose elfin features could easily be mistaken for those of a fairy, nodded.

"Well, that fair warms the cockles of me heart," Freya mimicked the lilting brogue, she had come to love. "Drinks all around," she waved her hand imperiously at Sean, who rolled his eyes, but set to, doing as she bade.

Observing the kindly faces surrounding her, and secure in Sean's devotion, Freya was not sure she would ever be able to leave.

EIGHT

Dublin was magnificent at any time of the year but at Christmas, it dazzled the senses. Decorated within an inch of its life and strewn with millions of lights, to Freya it was enchanting.

The celebration itself was not unknown to her, but Freya had never been in Midgard during the actual festivities.

Every chance she got, bundled up against the chill, she wandered the streets, captivated by the illuminations, the carols blaring from shop doorways, the food... especially the hot chocolate... and the cheerful window dressings.

Determined to embrace the season, the Norse goddess immersed herself in everything Christmas related, to the amusement of Sean and her friends at *The Oak Tree;* the latter of whom ribbed her mercilessly when she turned up wearing a bright red jumper covered with gingerbread men and be-ribboned candy canes.

"I like it." she stuck her nose in the air.

"You think this one is bad, wait until you see the one

with Rudolph on it, or the one with Christmas puddings." Sean pulled a truly gruesome face.

"No sense of fun, you people," Freya blew a raspberry — a gesture she had learned from Sela. "Now, barkeep, would you be so kind as to pour me a Guinness to sustain me as I finish trimming *your* tree, and while you're at it, is there any Shepherd's Pie?"

"Coming right up, your highness." Sean chuckled.

"And don't you forget it." She wagged a finger in amused admonishment.

She even allowed herself to be persuaded into attending church with Sean. While she found the service dignified and the congregation devout, the numerous statues were *not* to her fancy, and the choir left a lot to be desired — although what they lacked in harmony they made up for in exuberance.

Any excess tinsel, lights, and baubles ended up adorning Sean's house, which looked like a Christmas tree had exploded.

Not satisfied with making the interior resemble a fairy grotto, Freya scoured the shops to find ornaments to, as she declared, haughtily, "festivisize" the outside.

"Now you are just making up words to justify your addiction," Sean teased, shaking his head at the collection of snowmen, reindeer, and candy canes, scattered across the tiny front lawn. "I have a respectable reputation to uphold, you know."

"Pfft, who cares what your neighbors think? I love it."

She clasped her hands prayer-like to her chest and sighed. "As far as I can tell, this is the only time of the year you can allow your inner child to express itself, and I for one, believe it imperative we champion your traditions."

"Oh, well, if it's traditions you are interested in..." Sean let that trial off.

Freya spun to face him, detecting a devilish glint in his eye. Employing her true nature to maximum, if invisible, effect, she shimmied against him, her voice lowering seductively, "Go on."

Abruptly, he kissed her into breathlessness then, just as abruptly, stopped and opened the gate.

Freya snagged his jacket. "Hang on a minute, mister. What other traditions?"

"I'm tired. It's been a long day." Sean feigned a huge yawn. "Maybe another time."

He grinned at Freya's glower, enjoying the banter.

"Tell me." Ignoring the fact, they were standing in the street, in full view of said neighbors, Freya sought under layers of clothing, hearing Sean hiss when her cold fingers caressed his warm flesh.

"Ooof, not fair," Sean protested. "I cannot return the favor.

"You can't?" Freya raised an innocent brow.

"Geez, you are a minx," Sean shuddered when she tweaked the waistband of his jeans. He tried to grab her wandering hands but she was too quick for him.

"I know, but is it not delicious?" Freya chuckled wickedly. "Now tell me before I strip you naked and take you here on the pavement."

"You would not dare." Sean's chest rumbled with mirth.

Freya cocked her head, her eyes gleaming. "Want to bet?"

"Ok, you asked for it."

Before she realized what he was doing, he had hoisted her in a fireman's lift. Paying no heed to her squealed protests, he carried her into the house, feeling her small fists battering his back, in a futile attempt to force him to release her.

"Is that the best you've got?" he taunted, locking the door behind them.

"***Sean***," what Freya hoped would sound authoritative, came out as a gurgled squawk as he took advantage of her position to swat her butt.

"Sean." She tried again to no discernible effect and, all of a sudden, was laughing helplessly, every jolt as he pounded up the stairs, adding to her hilarity. "S-s-stop." She giggled. "I can't breathe."

He tossed her onto the bed, and shrugged out of his jacket to join her there.

Her amusement fled as he won the unspoken wager.

Later, much, much later, propped up on his elbow, Sean, one finger describing intricate designs over Freya's body, explained a few of the traditions adored by Dubliners and tourists alike. "You know the Twelve Days of Christmas?"

Freya had no idea what he was talking about but, not prepared to admit it, nodded.

"We added a twist, the Twelve Pubs of Christmas."

"Twelve Pubs?" Her nose crinkled in puzzlement. "What do you mean? One pub a day for twelve days? That's not much of a challenge?"

"Hahaha, not quite, it's twelve pubs in one night."

"Even that cannot be too hard, surely? There are plenty of pubs within easy walking distance of each other in Dublin."

"Ahhh, you're not wrong, but you haven't heard the rules?

Freya shuffled until she was on her side, and skewered him with a suspicious look. "Rules?"

He grinned. "One — participants must, and I cannot stress this enough, wear the most outrageous Christmas jumper they can find. Two — all other... err... accessories are encouraged—"

"Accessories?" Freya's eyebrows shot up to her hairline.

"You know, Santa hats, necklaces made of baubles, festive earrings... preferably ones that flash, things like that."

Freya sniggered. "Oh, we are definitely doing this."

"Hang on, you haven't heard the rest."

"Don't need to, seeing you all dolled up in a garish sweater and draped in tinsel is enough to persuade me it's a done deal."

"Fine, on your head be it. We ought to see who else might want to join us. It's way more fun with a group."

Freya rubbed her hands together in childish glee. "Oh, this is going to be juicy. When?"

"Hmmm, don't know until we check with the others. Now, given it's.... crap, two fifteen, and we have to be up in four hours, may I have the pleasure?"

He trailed a determined hand along the curve of her body.

Freya gasped as his fingers reached their goal. "Don't distract me," she husked. "I have things to plan," but didn't stop him.

"Oh, *mo chuisle,* as if I would."

Proceeding to do exactly that.

NINE

Four days before Christmas, Dublin, which had been unseasonably mild, was hit by an arctic blast. Temperatures plummeted and the world became white with frost, blanketed in beautiful but treacherous crystals.

Undeterred by the frigid weather, Freya had coaxed six of their friends to join Sean and her in the Twelve Pubs game.

Huddled around a table in *The Oak Tree*, they went through the rules, which ranged from the nonsensical to the absolutely ridiculous but, apparently, this was half the fun.

On top of the obvious, one drink in each pub, there were twelve more rules — one per bar.

At their first stop, every member of the group had to speak using a different foreign accent. No pointing in the next pub, no swearing in the third, and no talking in the fourth, singing everything at the fifth. The no names pub, the hug a stranger pub — the list went on.

Rule breakers paid a penalty which usually entailed drinking a shot of spirits.

If you made it to twelve, you patted yourself on the back — a feat made only vaguely possible by the amount of alcohol you had consumed in the previous eleven — and celebrated the fact you had made it to the end alive, that your liver had not, hopefully, suffered irreversible damage, and were... almost... upright.

They settled on the evening of the twenty-third for their shenanigans.

Christmas Eve was out of the question, being one the pub's busiest nights. Sean did not think it fair to expect his staff to work, while he gallivanted around getting sloshed.

The pub would close at midnight on the twenty-fourth and not reopen until lunchtime on the twenty-seventh, giving his loyal employees a well-earned break.

Attired in an array of outfits, so garish even the home-less would be forgiven for tossing them on a bonfire, the intrepid eight set out.

The streets were teeming with late night shoppers, partygoers, the usual revelers, people admiring the Christmas illuminations, and numerous other groups attempting the same challenge. Some of the latter doing it for charity, and taking photos as proof — which would, undoubtedly, become more blurred as the night wore on.

Hilarity increased in direct proportion to diminishing coherence.

Freya, although somewhat constrained by her *mortal* form, had discovered alcohol rarely affected her adversely.

Tonight, she wished she could experience a measure of drunkenness, to *feel* the buzz, the kick, her companions felt. To wallow in that glorious release of inhibitions... except the inevitable hangover, of course... *that* she was very happy to avoid.

Goddess of fertility, sex, lust, war, beauty, wealth, and abundance, she may well be, but right now she would relinquish them all for one evening of reckless inebriation — simultaneously acknowledging the repercussions would likely be catastrophic.

That said, Freya, who *did* become aware of a mild sense of fuzziness towards the end of the evening, was nothing if not a good actress, and none of her friends noticed she was scarcely even tipsy.

As they left the last pub...coincidentally, *The Oak Tree*, Freya became aware of a vaguely sour tang in the air and felt the brush of something light against her cheek. Glancing up, she realized it was snowing.

She hadn't seen snow for longer than she cared to count. Putting out her hand, she watched the delicate flakes land on her upturned palm, linger there momentarily, then evaporate in the heat from her skin.

"Sean," she murmured, for to speak any louder seemed... irreverent. "Look."

Everyone tilted their heads backwards to stare at the sky, entranced by the whirling flakes. Not necessarily the most sensible gesture when plastered. Several of them staggered, and Cormac would have fallen on his rear if not for Liam's steadying grip.

Silly giggles erupted. Freya shook her head, her lips twitching. They would be sorry for themselves in the morning.

"We'll have a white Christmas now," Aileen predicted, her words slurring slightly. "Kids'll be chuffed."

"Away home with yer," Sean encouraged. "Don't be dallying, it's already thickening." The least intoxicated...

outwardly, he flagged down a passing taxi, bundling in Liam, Cormac, and their wives, giving the driver directions, then doing the same for Neil, another regular, and his wife, Pippa.

"You ok to walk?" he asked Freya, draping an arm around her shoulders and pulling her flush to his side.

"Sure." Freya smiled. "It's not far."

In companionable silence, the couple strolled through the quiet streets, pausing occasionally to share a kiss, or admire a particularly impressive set of lights on a house.

Talking was unnecessary, and neither wanted to shatter the inexplicable hush which had descended, even the traffic noise was muffled.

By the time they reached the gate, the snow was a dizzying dance, turning the familiar into the unrecognizable.

"Just made it." Sean whistled through his teeth as he unlocked the front door, ushering Freya into the cozy warmth of the house ahead of him.

"Nightcap, or are you done?" he asked, taking her heavy winter jacket, shaking off the snow onto the tiled floor, and hanging it up.

"I think I'm done." Freya stretched, languidly and yawned. "Well, that was a night to remember. Although I fear our friends will not." She gurgled with laughter.

"I'm amazed you can still stand, never mind walk home." Sean chuckled. "You can certainly hold your liquor."

"Misspent youth," Freya said, kicking off her boots. She padded into the lounge and flopping on the capacious sofa, reclined against the cushions. "I am so sleepy." She closed her eyes and knew no more.

She had no recollection of being carried upstairs, divested of her clothes and various extras — including her tinsel-trimmed elf hat, which Sean thought ridiculously cute, and being tucked into bed.

Sean stood for several minutes staring down at her; glorious blonde hair splayed across the pillow, flawless porcelain skin, dark lashes describing a sooty curve over cheeks made rosy by the chill.

God, she is bewitching. His body reacted, surprising him, given the amount of alcohol he had imbibed.

In the pale glimmer from the streetlight creeping through the uncurtained window, she did not look quite real, as though she might vanish.

An odd creeping sensation trickled down his spine as, out of the blue, he recalled her seemingly random questions about the ancient ways and beliefs.

Then, Freya gave a little snore and he dismissed the half-formed notion as fanciful, induced by too many whiskeys. Shrugging out of his own clothes, he climbed in beside her, gathered her close and, in an instant, joined her in slumber.

Peeling open her eyes, Freya blinked, not quite sure what had woken her.

The curious light in the room suggested the dawn had broken, but something was not quite normal.

Levering herself up onto one elbow, she squinted at the window, over Sean's bulk.

The curtains were not drawn and, from what she could see of the sky... not much... it looked leaden. Her eyes swung to the clock perched on the cabinet next to Sean's side of the bed. The red digits glowed, a far too early, 8:15.

She lay back against the pillows and contemplated the

ceiling, her gaze following a faint crack in the plaster. Five minutes later, she swung her legs off the bed and got up.

Wrapping herself in Sean's enormous dressing gown, she walked over to the window.

She bit down on a shocked squeak. It was still snowing and had been very heavy overnight. Already several inches deep, the landscape was camouflaged in undulating whiteness. It was breathtaking.

A thrill ran through her and, careful not to disturb Sean, she pulled on the same clothes he had removed scant hours previously.

Tiptoeing down the stairs, she rugged up in her warm coat, boots, gloves, and scarf.

Unlocking the door, she turned the handle slowly, hearing the quiet click of the latch, and swung it open. Cold air rushed in to meet her, making her gasp.

Involuntarily, she shivered but nothing was going to prevent her from stepping into the pristine world.

Everything was eerily silent. There was no breeze, no sounds of birdsong, not even the usual hum of cars.

She stood on the path. The garden ornaments had become shapeless blobs, although Rudolph's red nose was just visible through the layer of flakes.

She scanned the street... no one else was abroad... *no one else was crazy enough,* she grinned to herself.

Freya went out of the gate, and walked along to the park on the corner, trudging through the deepening snow.

It was as though she was the only person on the whole planet.

She glanced back, seeing her footsteps, a solitary, if winding, trail behind her. "This must be how explorers feel when they stumble across land, undiscovered until that moment," she said, oddly awed by the sensation.

She made her way to the swing set, brushed the snow from the plastic seat, and sat down, moving back and forth, idly, watching the ceaseless swirl of snowflakes.

Shortly thereafter, Sean appeared, shoulders hunched against the cold. "What on earth possessed you to leave a warm bed, and an even warmer Irishman to come sit on a frozen swing?"

He grinned as he bent to kiss her. "Good morning."

"I couldn't help it. I was lured by winter's magic." She smiled up at him, unaware of how enchanting she looked. "How did you know I was here?"

He jerked his head the way he had come. "Followed your footsteps... literally."

She glanced beyond him at the pockets of disturbed snow, marking their tracks. For some reason, their very randomness in so unmarred a scene made her giggle.

Circling the large metal frame, Sean came to stand behind Freya and pushed the swing lazily. He stared down at her, wondering whether she would object if he suggested they threw caution to the winds and made love in the snow. *To see her alabaster skin freckled with snowflakes...*

"Snowball fight?" he asked by way of distracting his indecent thoughts, already picking up a handful of snow and patting it between his palms.

Freya knitted her brows, scouring her brain for clarification of his question, coming up blank.

Surely a person purporting to hail from Norway ought to know everything about snow.

Before she could ask, the answer came in the form of an icy smack in the face.

"You stinking rotter," she spluttered indignantly, particles of snow sneaking down her neck. "You're going to regret that."

"You have to catch me first," Sean replied, dancing about a few feet away.

It was on.

Neither gave the other any quarter, hurling ball after ball of fluffy snow at the other, their laughter filling the air.

Eventually, Freya fell on her knees, and threw up her hands.

"I surrender," she panted dramatically, convulsed with mirth, collapsing backwards into the snow. "Oh, this is an interesting angle." She stuck her tongue out, tasting the cobweb-like flakes.

Sean plowed his way towards her and stretched out his hand to haul her upright. Freya gripped it and jerked hard, pulling him down into the thick carpet of white.

"Not fair," he complained. "Now we're both stuck." Doing nothing about their predicament. "Have you ever made a snow angel?"

Freya stilled. *Snow angels?*

"How do you know of snow creatures?" The question was out before she could stop it. "I thought they were confined to Niflheim."

"Niflheim? Is that some town in Lapland, near Santa's grotto?" Sean quizzed, only half-seriously.

Registering her mistake, Freya thought rapidly, and replied as casually... and as truthfully... as possible, "Yes, right at the northern tip, an almost mythical place really. Very remote.

"Legend has it that all ice creatures come from there. The kind of place parents threaten to send their children if they are misbehaving."

"So, a bit like monsters under the bed, or trolls under bridges?"

Freya sat up in the snow, resembling, so Sean thought, a

winter princess. Snow clung to her hair, her clothes, even her eyelashes.

"We need to go home, this stuff looks nice and fluffy but it soon seeps through your clothes. Last thing you need is to catch a chill."

Freya did not feel it pertinent to apprise him of that impossibility. "Before we do, tell me about snow angels?"

"Easier to show you." Sean grinned and lay back in the snow, sweeping his arms in a semi-circle from his sides to the top of his head creating an arc of flattened snow. He pushed himself upright and pointed at the hollow where he had been lying.

"See… snow angel."

Scrambling to her feet, Freya stared, then gave a smoth-ered whoop and dropped back to the ground to copy Sean's action.

Standing, she admired their efforts, her smaller angel alongside his huge one… he really was very brawny.

"His and Hers," she crowed, somewhat giddy with relief that Sean had not pressed her about Niflheim.

Problem was the longer she spent in Ireland, the more convinced she became that the gods, or at least the other-worldly, were present, all around them every day, not some half-forgotten relic of the past.

CHAPTER

TEN

Once the mad rush of Christmas Eve was over, the couple spent the next two days quietly. The snow continued to fall, although it was becoming sporadic, until Boxing Day when, finally, the sun came out.

The monochromatic world transformed into myriad shades of white and everything seemed to sparkle.

The air remained frigid, the meager warmth of the sun unable to break the icy grip but, as New Year loomed, the temperatures rose marginally and the snow began to melt... to Freya's abject disappointment.

"I wish it could stay all year," she moaned to Sean, as they walked to work, two days after Christmas.

Hmmm... Freya... do not dare to trick me into creating a mini-ice-age, her brother's voice castigated in her mind.

She bit down on a grin, *Worth a try.*

Ignoring the tutting reverberating in her head, she turned her attention back to Sean, who was asking her something.

"Of course, whatever you think." she essayed hoping that covered a multitude of questions.

"You agree?" He frowned.

Dammit, to what am I agreeing? Freya had a second's misgiving. "Sorry, run that by me again."

Sean squeezed her arm, hooked through his for balance on the icy paths more than anything, although she *did* enjoy the contact.

"I thought a New Year's Party at the bar might be fun. I don't usually bother, there are so many other pubs doing it, but well, you're here and..." he stopped.

"Wait, you want to have this party in my honor?" Freya quizzed.

A faint red stain washed up Sean's cheeks, and he nodded almost shyly. "Well, we didn't have one at Christmas because we did the twelve pubs, and it's your first New Year in Dublin... I think it deserves more than a glass of Guinness."

"You are quite the knight, Sean Kavanagh. It sounds lovely."

"Themed?" Sean risked.

Freya rolled her eyes, but had no intention of dousing the light in his eyes. Making him wait until they reached the museum, she gave a long, resigned sigh. "If we must."

Then squeaked when he swung her into his arms for a searing kiss.

"My good man, you have no shame."

"I know." He gave a wicked grin, released her, and walked off towards *The Oak Tree,* leaving her breathless on the pavement.

Sean did not advertise the New Year's celebrations as much as mentioned it to the regulars, and stood an easily missed notice on the bar.

When Freya asked why he was not posting flyers for it in the windows, he shrugged, saying he preferred to keep it low key and among friends rather than have hordes of rowdy revelers descending on them and causing uproar.

"I thought that was the whole point?" Freya raised a puzzled brow.

"Maybe for some, but for me, saying goodbye to the old year and welcoming the new should be with those you know, not strangers. To be sure, they'll all be drunk as lords by kicking out time, but in a more respectful manner." He winked, adding, "They damage me bar, I know where the buggers live, can't say the same for them as I've never met."

"That did not occur to me. You're not as green as you are cabbage looking." She tapped his chest cheekily.

"Where on earth did you hear that gem?" Sean did not think the phrase had made it all the way to Scandinavia.

"Liam." She grinned. "I like it."

"Now why does that not surprise me. Ok... themes, food, and deccies."

Freya thought for a moment. "How about an homage to Ireland? You have all that — what do you call it, bunting? — in the back. We still have the tree and the Christmas lights. String up the bunting and we're done. That covers the decorations.

"Food... finger food would be the easiest option. Maybe some jacket potatoes filled with cheese or stew if people want something more substantial. Perhaps an Irish themed cocktail. Are there liqueurs in green, orange, and white? Mind that might be dangerous."

"Fear not, there are plenty of Irish cocktails, although I might experiment." Sean ruminated, his mind whirring.

"Will you need help preparing the food?" Freya had proved herself a dab hand in the kitchen, although, if she deigned to help out at the pub, she preferred serving drinks... *she was a goddess after all*.

"Full staff on that night. We'll be fine. Thank you for offering though, I know how much you *adore* mundane tasks," Sean teased.

Freya jabbed an elbow in his ribs. "Watch it, mister."

"Ooof, no need for violence."

"Fancy dress?" Freya tossed out for good measure.

Sean clutched his head theatrically. "Do we have to?"

"No but I shall call you a party-pooper all night if we don't."

"I really must have a quiet word with Liam," Sean acquiesced with a comical grimace.

The couple fell into their usual banter as they finalized the details.

New Year's Eve dawned sunny with a clear blue sky. Still cold, but the biting wind had dropped and, although much of the snow had yet to thaw, the paths and roads were clear.

Freya finished her shift at the museum, and strolled around to the pub, edging her way through the reasonably large crowd already gathered. Tara waved, lifted a half-pint of Guinness, and nodded towards the only free table in the far corner of *The Snug*.

"It's so busy?" Freya smiled at Tara accepting the glass, gratefully. "Thank you for this." She took a long sip, then licked the film of foam off her top lip. "So good."

"It's crazy. You'd think we're the only pub open in the whole o' Dublin." Tara shook her head, collecting a stack of crockery and wedging it against her hip, while she wiped the table. "It'll thin out soon."

"I presumed the party would be private?"

"It will be, Sean has it under control." Tara glanced at the tall Irishman chatting with a couple of punters while pulling pints, unaware her eyes could not hide her feelings.

Freya caught the look and stored it away for future reference.

The theme had been embraced with almost as much enthusiasm as the cocktails. Sean had even managed to create a drink with Creme de Menthe and Aperol topped with a layer of cream to imitate the colors of the Irish flag. No one noticed that the arrangement of the layers didn't match the stripes on the flag, and declared the orange-minty flavor to be delicious.

Using the museum to her advantage, Freya had done her research, and modeled her costume on depictions of the goddess Danu, who — according to legend — was the mother to a race of supernatural beings. In Freya's opinion... a fitting choice.

Despite her diminutive stature, with her pale blonde hair and dainty features, the flowing, medieval gown gave her an ethereally regal appearance as she circulated among the patrons, carrying platters of hors d'oeuvres. More than one commented on how well the outfit suited her.

Freya kept her counsel.

Sean — who had opted to dress as a leprechaun, an hilarious choice given his imposing height — stayed behind the bar. "Safest place," he had said to Freya when she questioned him on it.

There were five other staff working alongside them, so

no one was ever without refreshment of one form or another.

Now, the bar was empty save Sean and Freya. Midnight with its tradition of first footing, a forgotten hour.

The party had been acclaimed, by all and sundry, to be a huge success, not that most would remember it the next morning.

Tired, and a little tipsy, Freya perched on the bar swinging her legs, while Sean cashed up and stowed everything in the safe.

"Want another drink?" he asked, coming through from the office and locking the door. "It's New Year's Day, worthy of celebration."

"I think we've celebrated enough tonight to last the rest of the year." She grinned rather woozily. "Kiss me."

"Hmmm... demanding kisses are we now. Not sure—"

For the life of him, Sean could not fathom how he got from behind the bar to the front; positive he had not actually walked. *Too many cocktails,* he thought.

"Are ye sure ye not related to Áine?" he murmured not altogether coherently.

"Who is this is Áine?" Freya asked, as her slender fingers tiptoed down his unbuttoned, emerald-green waistcoat, to twitch his shirt out of the matching trousers.

"Queen of the Fairies, a powerful and beautiful goddess. Ooof... have you had those fingers in an ice bucket," he rasped as Freya's hands swarmed over his back, their gentle pressure drawing him closer.

Fairy-folk and goddesses... again. She ignored it for the moment, more important things taking precedence.

"I'm naturally cool." She scattered featherlight kisses along his jaw line, to the soft shell of his ear, grazing her teeth against the tender lobe. Hooking her legs around his waist, she pulled him to her, their bodies meeting and melding.

As though she was the finest crystal, Sean lowered Freya until her back was flush with the bar, then followed her over, his lips teasing and tormenting while his hands sought under the frothy layers of her gown, to stroke along the inside of her thigh, brushing her heat.

Freya wriggled, desperate for him to weave his spell. "Is the front door locked," the last word soaring up an octave and her back bowed as his fingers reached their goal.

"Of course," the answer rumbled in her ear. "Now hush."

For once, Freya did as she was told.

"About that drink," Sean reminded, some considerable time later.

Freya stretched, languidly, and suppressed a yawn. "Why not? What do you suggest?"

How about a shot of this?" He pushed himself to his feet and walked around the bar. Unlatching one of the cupboards tucked away underneath the polished bench, he withdrew a bottle containing green liquid.

In the dim glow from the only two wall lamps still switched on, Freya squinted at the label. "Absinthe? Never heard of it."

"Oh, *mo chuisle,* then you must try it."

"It is very... err... green." Freya grasped the bottle and unscrewed the lid. Gingerly, she sniffed as the aroma drifted into the air. "Anise..." she cocked her head, "...or fennel, hmmm... lemon balm?" she asked, discerning several other botanicals, whose names eluded her.

"Wow, good nose, all three." Sean was impressed.

"I know."

"And so modest." He laughed. "Okay, so it's too strong to drink undiluted..."

"I would like to try a sip, neat first."

"Freya," he took the bottle from her, "this stuff is like seventy percent proof. Could kill yer."

"I sincerely doubt it. I only want a teeny taste." She batted her eyelashes at him and assumed her most winsome expression.

"Fine, but let me pour it." He was putty in her hands when she did that. Measuring out what looked like three drops in a shot glass, he slid it across the bar.

The bitter bouquet coiled up her nostrils, to settle at the back of her throat. There was something... an ancientness to this spirit, the fragrance alone able to summon up the past. Freya let a drop sit on her tongue, the warmth of the black liquorice flavor counteracting the initial sharpness.

She felt the punch of the alcohol content and coughed slightly. It was definitely strong, but not unpleasant.

"I warned you," Sean said.

"Actually, I like it, but will bow to your suggestion that I drink the rest diluted." She smiled.

She watched Sean retrieve two sugar cubes from the jar they were stored in. A dash of absinthe went into a cocktail glass, over which he balanced a teaspoon with one of the sugar cubes. Iced water was then dripped over the cube slowly until it had dissolved.

Adding a decent splash of water to the syrupy mixture, he gave it a quick stir, then repeated the ritual with the second glass.

"A tad complicated," Freya mused.

"But worth it."

Sean set the two drinks alongside each other. The water

had turned the bright green liquor cloudy, adding to its mystique.

"The main ingredient is wormwood," Sean explained as they clinked their glasses and sipped. "Goes back to biblical times. In fact, it's been associated with gods and magic since before then, but it was a much simpler formula, and more curative than a drink for pleasure."

Again, he talks of the gods and their powers. Freya thought. *Too many coincidences.*

"It's commonly known as the Green Fairy because of the green anise, or maybe because people profess to have seen a green fairy after drinking it neat. Who knows?" Sean chuckled. "Interchangeable with Green Lady or Green Goddess."

He straightened up and lifted his glass in a kind of flourish. "To quote Aleister Crowley, a crazy bloke who wrote a book about absinthe, 'Ah, the Green Goddess. What is the fascination that makes her so adorable and so terrible?' *Mo mhuirnín,* looking at yer wearing that stunning dress, I reckon you are my goddess." He bowed. "Or perhaps Áine."

When she looked back on it, Freya could not, for the life of her... and it was a very, *very* long life, recall what triggered her reaction.

She suspected it was a combination of several things, not least the constant references to magic and myth, gods and goddesses, queens and fairy-folk, legends, and antiquity.

She blamed Sean... who, once he had recovered from the shock, blamed himself as well.

*Never, **ever** trust the Green Fairy.*

She slid off the barstool, shook out the sleeves of her gown and discarded her earthly form, transforming into

Freya, most revered female deity of the Norse pantheon, ruler of Fólkvangr, goddess of love, beauty, fertility, sex, war, gold, and divination.

Thinking it would amuse Sean, she allowed her inner light to glow green instead of silver.

"F-Fr-*Freya*? What the fuck?" Gawking, Sean rocked on his heels and almost fell over, grabbing the edge of the bar to steady himself. He blinked rapidly, certain he had fallen asleep and this was a dream... or maybe a nightmare. *Bloody absinthe... wait, I've only had a mouthful.*

She spoke, and her voice had a peculiar resonance. "Sean Kavanagh, I am Freya of Fólkvangr, kneel before me." Accompanying her command with an impish smile.

Sean was held immobile, his eyes all but popping out of his head. Had his life depended on it, he would not have moved a single inch. He could not even breathe.

In a split-second, the glow vanished and Freya was cupping his jaw. She pressed a kiss to his frozen lips and a scene from a fairy tale skittered through his mind... only this was in reverse.

"Sean, are you okay?"

Air rushed out of his lungs and he sank on to the nearest barstool, his heart hammering. He coerced his mouth to connect to his brain. "What the actual fuck was that?"

Freya took a step backwards, her smile faded, supplanted by confusion. "It was just me."

A hard knot formed under her breast.

You stupid fool, she chastised herself, inwardly. *Now you've gone and ruined what could be the best thing ever to happen to you. Why do you always have to ruin things?*

Her usual confidence deserted her, and she moved away

from him, muttering a slew of curses in ancient Norse at her ineptitude.

"Forgive me, I should not have, but... you seemed... it was... because..." coherence already teetering on the brink — in part owing to the amount of alcohol she had consumed, but more to the sudden glut of emotions flooding her consciousness — abandoned her completely.

For the first time in millennia, tears brimmed in her astonishing blue eyes. Angrily, she swiped them away and turned to leave, only to turn back.

She had to put this right. The repercussions of witnessing a transcendental shift could be far reaching and Sean's mind might never recover.

He did not deserve that.

About to replace the paranormal with something less... controversial and infinitely more temporal, she composed herself.

"Freya." Sean's voice penetrated her distress.

She shook her head and began the chant.

"Freya," he repeated, rubbing his forehead distractedly. "Stop with the incantation, and come here."

She suspended the spell, but did not move. She did not fear Sean's wrath, she did not fear his strength — she could smite him dead in an instant.

What she feared was his revulsion; that the tenderness in his gaze would dwindle, replaced by blank indifference.

She was trembling. Never in her entire existence had she trembled. Not even when Odin blew his stack.

Numerous, seemingly insignificant remarks, questions, details coalesced in Sean's brain and the picture, while unimaginable, inconceivable, and implausible, suddenly made sense.

Yes, this was big, huge... okay, bloody enormous but, when push came to shove, it was quite simple really.

He loved Freya. Didn't matter who... or what... she was. He loved her. He had never felt this way about anyone, and doubted such a depth of emotion would happen again.

He had two choices. Walk away or walk towards her.

He closed the gap, and seized her hand, gathering her to him, feeling the tremors rippling through her svelte frame.

"Freya, I have no damn clue what just happened or who you are, although, goddess would not be far-fetched. I think we share something special, something rare, something which comes along once, maybe twice in a lifetime. I do not want to miss it."

He ran a light finger under her chin, tilting it until she met his eyes. What she saw in their emerald depths was more eloquent than any words.

She sighed, and it seemed to come from the far reaches of the universe... and, given her recent revelation... not without merit.

Sean kissed her.

ELEVEN

Freya leaned into Sean, and kissed him back with a kind of desperation, pressed a hand to his cheek, spun around, and fled into the night... uncaring that she used her magic to pass through a locked door.

Despite what she had seen in Sean's gaze, she just needed to escape.

Not easy when you live with the guy.

She hovered on the curb, uncertainly, wondering where to go. The hotel was close by, it would only take her minutes to get there.

She had barely crossed the road when she heard footsteps behind her. She did not have to look to know it was Sean. Ever practical, he had slung on his jacket and was carrying her coat.

"Freya, *mo chuisle,* where d'yer think yer going? It's the middle of the night and you're in fancy dress." Dry humor laced his question.

"Sean..." She put up her hands as though to fend him off.

Giving her no chance to argue, or send him away, or

disappear, he draped her coat around her shoulder, and as he had in the pub, wrapped his arms around her, and held her close.

She stiffened, and for a moment, he thought she might push him away. Imperceptibly, she relaxed, although Sean sensed she could give him the slip without warning.

Their relationship hung on a knife edge, and he knew a fraught conversation was in the offing; not least that it seemed his — what was she? — partner... woman... mate was not of this earth. In itself enough to blow your mind.

Why *wasn't* his mind blown?

Sean registered that, despite being confronted by *the* most outlandish scenario, he wasn't fazed. His feelings for Freya transcended all logic and reason.

Time slid by unnoticed and, as they stood in the middle of the street, cloaked in darkness, the snow began to fall again. Delicate flakes drifting down to dust the couple and the ground around them.

"Sean, what do those words mean?" Freya whispered, unwilling to shatter the hush.

Sean canted his head to study her. "Okay, fair enough. *Mo chuisle* actually means my pulse, but between couples it's more like the beat of my heart. *Mo mhuirnín,* is me darlin' or sweetheart, and *mo chroí* means my heart." The lilting Gaelic sounded like a melody.

Under the glare of the streetlamp, Freya caught that tell-tale red stain — so rare in this burly Irishman whom, she swore, had Viking ancestry — washing up his face.

"I did not intend to freak you out. I know, well I can imagine how you f—"

"Can you? That was some bombshell you just dropped."

There was a long pause. Freya rested her forehead

against his chest and inhaled his scent, an intoxicating blend of man and cologne.

"Actually, no, I cannot and, I daresay you want an explanation."

"First sensible thing you've said all day." There was no rancor in his voice.

"Hey, no need to be rude. It was a momentary lapse..." she peeked up at him, and gripped the lapels of his leather jacket, her thumbs burrowing into the warm sheepskin lining. "Sean, I'm—"

"You're my Green Goddess. Now, I get we are going to have to deal with this...err... startling... errr... exposé but, how about we put it on the back burner 'til the morning. It's cold, it's very late, or rather early, and we're tired.

"Things always look better after a good night's sleep.

"If, after you've told me what the hell all this is about, we decide staying together is untenable then, so be it. Not tonight. You look like a gust of wind would knock you flat. What d'yer reckon?"

Said gust of wind whistled along the empty street, making Freya shiver.

Reluctantly, aware she was only prolonging the inevitable, she capitulated. She really didn't want to explain to James or Maeve or whoever happened to be on reception at the hotel, why she needed a room at stupid o'clock on New Year's Day. She had her dignity to consider... blithely ignoring the fact, *that* had gone out of the window about an hour ago.

"Okay, on your head be it."

Sean flashed her a grin, his teeth gleaming white in the darkness. "Come on then, let's go home.

When they arrived home, despite Sean's suggestion of the benefits of a good night's sleep, going to bed seemed... awkward. By tacit consent, he lit the fire, while Freya made hot chocolate, and they curled up on the sofa.

Refusing to allow Freya to retreat into her shell, Sean encouraged her to "spill the beans..." which required immediate clarification, because Freya took him literally.

Her misunderstanding of the popular phrase reminded him how often this had happened. He had always assumed it was simply nuances of language but now, he realized, it related to lack of association with mortals.

Listen to yerself, Sean, he rolled his eyes inwardly. *Mortals, my arse. She's got yer talking like her.* He allowed himself a grin.

Freya, after a protracted silence when she had tried... and failed... to corral wayward thoughts, decided to be blunt. Beating around the bush was futile with Sean; he was too astute. So, she gave him an honest, if abridged, account of her life from the first time she recalled existing.

"Wait, you're telling me, you're pretty much as old as time... looking good for your age, by the way... you can swan around the world in some kind of magical carriage pulled by two cats? Cats? Really, you couldn't have chosen something a tad more regal, like... oh, I don't know... a panther?"

Sean paced up and down the living room, ticking things off on his fingers.

"You have a multitude of powers, can disguise yourself as anyone you want, and are immortal... well, if I accept the first point, that's obvious." he slapped his forehead.

"What about the movies? The ones with Thor and Loki, are they..."

"Based on truth?" For the first time since this discussion started, in fact, for the first time since she had betrayed herself, Freya laughed, she couldn't help it. The golden sound, like a chime of bells, was music to Sean's ears. "What do you reckon?"

The tension in the room dissipated.

He stopped pacing to sit next to her. While this woman... goddess... had more strength in her little finger than the rest of the world put together, right at this moment, she looked unutterably fragile. Her eyes were huge in her white face, and she was chewing her lip.

He studied her pinched features, and it dawned on him how hard this must be for her too. To have no alternative but to hide your true nature every minute of every day, must be exhausting, yet her behavior, her demeanor gave nothing away.

To the average person, she was just Freya Lothbrok, who volunteered at the museum, helped out at the bar — age indeterminate.

A new thought struck him, and his lips twitched. Oh, this was gold... or green or silver... whatever hue she preferred.

"Now, what's tickled you?" Freya pinned him with wary blues.

"Nothing really, I was just thinking, given the age difference, which, let's face it, is vast... I'm basically your toy boy."

She frowned, uncomprehendingly.

Sean explained the term. "I'm fine with it by the way..." he drew out the word 'fine'. "Also makes you a cougar... maybe even the first cougar."

Thanks to Sela and her addiction to trashy television shows, Freya knew *precisely* what this meant, and she punched Sean in the shoulder.

"You cheeky bugger." Her smile softened her censure.

She pondered the moniker and her smile widened. "I admit, the notion sits well with me, but utter a word about this to a single other soul and it will be the last thing you do."

"What, that you are a goddess or a cougar?"

"Yes."

TWELVE

evelations of Freya's — for want of a better word —
heritage, and subsequent adjustment to her arcane
alchemy aside, the couple's relationship flourished. To Sean's own surprise, he discovered his sense of
shock was less traumatic than it ought to have been.

He conceded that the normal reaction would be to have
Freya committed to a lunatic asylum, but could not deny
what he had seen. It was not some crazy tale he had overheard, it was a phenomenon he had witnessed.

Perhaps growing up in a land steeped in myth and
legend had left him more receptive to the fantastical,
recalling a conversation in the pub one night about the fae
and magic.

Whatever the reason, he accepted Freya's unique *char-
acteristics*, with nary so much as a blink. *We're none of us
perfect*, he had justified inwardly. *Everyone is allowed their
idiosyncrasies*.

Occasionally, he *did* question whether this whole thing
was a dream... one which would beat a certain shower

scene starring Bobby Ewing, hollow. Then Freya would kiss him, obliterating the possibility.

As winter crept towards spring, they found a new balance, their feelings becoming more profound.

Sean knowing was a game changer for Freya. This is not to say she permitted him to see her as anything other than flawless — she was too vain for that but, being able to relax in the haven of their home without fear of exposing aspects of her immense power, was a huge relief.

Not to mention it also allowed her to 'recharge her batteries' — in a metaphysical sense.

Sean rarely referred to her otherworldliness, content life had reverted... almost... to the status quo.

To outward appearances, Freya was the same person she had always been — sassy, vivacious, and impish. She continued to volunteer at the museum, and help out at *The Oak Tree* if they were short staffed. She ran the pub quiz, and oversaw the darts games.

Not a single person other than Sean could have guessed what simmered beneath the surface.

A state of affairs, Freya was not about to revise.

"You cannot keep this boy," the sneering voice boomed around her head.

"Give me one good reason why," Freya hissed, outraged that Odin had the audacity to enter her dreams.

"He is mortal, you are not. You are embarrassing yourself and your status by consorting with so puny a male. Hear me... if you continue on this ludicrous path, his life will be forfeit."

"You have no call to interfere in this realm." Ice slithered down Freya's spine.

"You know the whelp is going to confess his undying love for you. He has hovered on the brink several times. Once he utters those words, you cannot save him."

"Odin, listen to yourself. You cannot usurp the rules pertaining to Midgard."

"Do not push me, Freya. You are as much at fault for pursuing this ridiculous liaison as he is for falling under your spell. You know better. Your persistent dalliances with that reprobate Loki were pathetic, this is just pitiful."

Odin's implacable tone left Freya in no doubt, he would carry out his threat.

"He is an innocent,

Odin. What possible reason could you have for harming him? He has done nothing to warrant your wrath."

"He is human. Your desire to procreate has blinded your common sense. You cannot sully the bloodline."

"*Sully the bloodline...*" Freya retorted scornfully, her voice rising at least one octave in righteous indignation. "What is it about *this* man? Why not any of my other paramours whom you so delightfully disparage every chance you get?"

"This time you have allowed your heart to rule your head. You are a laughing stock in Valhalla. Freya, the Goddess of Sex and Seduction, brought to her knees... by a mere mortal." His derisive laughter reverberated in her mind and she fought to expel his presence... to little effect.

"You cannot hide from me, Freya. Remember we are handfasted. It is time you returned to your own realm. Come home. Forget the human."

"F... get out of my head, old man." Freya swallowed the expletive so beloved of mortals, refusing to grant Odin the satisfaction of knowing he had riled her. "What I do with my life is none of your business."

The cruel laughter grew louder. "So naive. I have said my piece. Do not linger in Midgard, Freya, the consequences will be... let us just say... lamentable..."

Odin's cackling faded, drowned out by another voice.

"Freya, wake up, you're having a nightmare. *Freya*..."

Climbing up through layers of sleep, Freya batted at the hands shaking her.

"Hey, watch it." Amusement laced the tones of the speaker. Her bunched fists were grasped and she felt cool lips brush a kiss to her hot face. "Don't want you punching me into another dimension."

That jolted Freya awake and she bolted upright. The room was in darkness.

"S-Sean..."

"You expecting someone else?"

Freya stared at him, committing his arresting features to memory, while she tried and failed to come up with a pert response. Taking refuge in running trembling fingers through her disheveled hair, she muttered. "Sorry, bad dream."

"You're telling me, you were like an angry octopus. Wanna tell me about it?"

"N-not right now. What time is it?"

"Dunno." Sean peered over her shoulder. "Just after four."

"Too early to be awake." Freya snuggled against him more for comfort than anything else. His arms came around her, and her erratic heartbeat steadied. He pressed his lips to the top of her head.

Moments later they were both fast asleep... this time without dreams.

As spring banished the last of winter, Freya tried to banish Odin's threat; tried to persuade herself the damn Asgardian had not invaded her slumber.

For a while, it worked.

The beauty of spring in Dublin provided a temporary distraction.

Trees, once stark and dormant, sprouted buds in every shade of green imaginable. Gossamer veils became silken cloaks as the tiny leaves unfurled. a profusion of flowers bloomed to carpet the ground, and birds zipped about, singing lustily as they collected material for their nests.

The museum was bustling. Although the holiday season in Dublin was, more or less, year-round, spring always brought an extra influx of visitors. Freya's days were long and tiring, but rewarding. She never lost the joy of imparting knowledge, watching a sea of avid faces soak it up.

The Oak Tree was equally busy. Its location, just off Westmoreland Street, along with its historical façade, made it a popular watering hole for tourists.

The days merged into one, their exhausting routine leaving no time for introspection.

Yet, Freya's heart ached.

Her time in this sanctuary was coming to an end. It was as clear as the exquisitely illuminated letters in the Book of Kells, but Freya was torn. She was not ready to say goodbye to Sean... she did not think she would ever be ready.

Despite her best efforts, her almost imperceptible with-drawal did not go unnoticed by Sean. Sensitive to every nuance where Freya was concerned, he knew something had shifted.

One night, as they curled up together on the sofa after a hectic day, he broached the subject.

"What's going on, Freya?"

Freya did not waste her breath asking what he meant, and steeled herself to be honest. He did not deserve prevarication. "If I stay here with you, your life is in danger."

Sean did not laugh, although had he been sitting next to anyone else, the bald statement would seem like a bad joke. He rested his head on top of hers and stroked gentle fingers up and down her arm.

"Care to explain that?"

There was a lengthy silence. Through the open window, the breeze rustled the trees and, over the distant hum of traffic, an owl hooted. Restful sounds, familiar sounds, sounds of home.

Freya felt as though she was being ripped to shreds.

"Odin has summoned me, demanding I return to Fólkvangr."

"Why does he care what you do?"

"He does not, but has an aversion to me being happy."

Sean recalled Freya's nightmare, and her disinclination to tell him about it. "Is this something to do with that dream you had a few weeks back?"

She huffed a sigh. "It is. It was not so much a dream, as Odin deeming it time he paid me a visit, to remind me of my *obligations*," Freya all but spat the last word. She gave Sean a synopsis of her conversation with the All Father.

"He knows how close we have become. He knows you are on the verge of declaring the strength of your feelings, and it galls him."

Not privy to the machinations of the Gods — who in

this realm was? — especially Odin, Sean knew he ought to be confounded by her words but, when it came to Freya, nothing seemed out of the ordinary.

"I am at a loss. What does our relationship matter to some grizzled god?"

"He sees me as his. I refuse to pander to his will, which has led to him deciding that if he can't have me no one can."

"Hence the 'your life is in danger,' comment."

"Exactly." Freya twisted in the seat to face Sean. One hand caressed his jaw, light fingers tracing his ear before cupping his nape. Their foreheads touched.

"I have never cared for anyone, the way I care for you and, for that very reason, I must leave. Odin will not permit you to steal my heart."

"Mo gh—" Sean started, only to have Freya's fingertips stop him uttering the endearment.

"Please do not say it. I know and your sentiment is returned, but our mutual affection cannot be enunciated. It will likely be the last thing you ever do, and I cannot risk it." She tilted her head and their lips met. Their smoldering passion ignited.

"Then, if our time together is running out, we'd do well not to squander it." Sean swung her into his arms and carried her upstairs, where he proceeded to ensure she would never forget him.

Three weeks later, the perfect excuse — in the guise of an invitation addressed to Freya and accompanied by a begging letter — landed on Sean's doormat.

Freya,

Yes, it's finally happening. We're getting married (I know you can't see but, I am dancing a wild jig here). Please, please come home to be my maid of honor, it will not be the same if you are not part of the celebrations.

Freya read on, noting the date, which was less than a fortnight away.

She sent out a heartfelt thank you to Sela, for providing a 'get out' clause, instantly forgiving her friend for the numerous occasions when she had driven her batty, and almost exonerating Sela for snagging Loki right out from under her nose.

She gave the museum two weeks' notice. Yes, she was a volunteer with no cause to do anything other than to inform them of her decision but, it was high season, and it was not fair nor polite to walk away without forewarning.

They were sorry to see her go and, even though she did not mix outside work hours, Freya had proved to be an invaluable member of their cohort. The farewell card signed by everyone in her department, and the little gift... a silver, Celtic knot brooch... reduced her to tears.

She didn't tell anyone at *The Oak Tree,* either that she had quit the museum or that she was leaving. She did not possess the strength to parry the litany of questions she knew would be flung at her, nor did she want to lie when asked about her return.

Hiding her imminent departure from Sean was the hardest thing she had ever done, and her final few days with him were bittersweet. She wanted them to last forever as much as she wanted them to be over. The emotion neither had confessed, swirled around them, so potent it was almost tangible.

Heartbreak was new to Freya. She had been bruised by love, frustrated by love, battered by love, and had found love to be a royal pain in the behind, but, until this moment, her heart had remained intact.

She could not say goodbye to Sean. She could not tell him these hours were the last they would spend together. She could not bear to see the grief in his eyes, knowing it was mirrored in hers.

So, she took the coward's way out.

She wrote an eloquent letter, in which she poured out her feelings and explained why it had to be this way. Then, she folded it neatly, slid it into an envelope and, as women have done for centuries, sealed it with a kiss.

Obstinately determined to add to her own misery, Freya decided to travel to New York by conventional means. That this would delay her arrival, merely a fortuitous bonus.

She bought a business-class ticket for a flight departing in three days and, while Sean was at work, packed her few belongings into a suitcase, small enough to be considered hand luggage.

The night prior to Freya's departure, and despite the fact, she had not told Sean she was leaving the following morning, it was as though he had read her mind. They came together in an almost desperate frenzy, their bodies screaming the words they dared not avow.

Woken by the dawn chorus, Freya lay for hours just watching Sean, committing every adored feature to her mind. Unwilling to cause him any more sadness, she cushioned the sense of loss, she knew he would feel, by planting the vaguest inkling of a possibility into his mind.

It might take a little while to germinate — one did not recover from losing a goddess overnight — but when it blossomed, his soul would smile once more.

Which is more than Freya expected of her own.

By sheer force of will, she dragged herself out of bed, managing to shower and dress without disturbing Sean.

Half an hour later, suitcase in hand, she crept from the house she had grown to love as much as the man within.

When she reached the gate, Freya turned, stared up at the window, and murmured, "*Slan leat, mo ghrá.*" The Irish she had practiced for this very moment closing a chapter of her life.

Farewell, my love.

It took everything she had to walk away.

CHAPTER
THIRTEEN

Freya's plane sat at its gate for the fourth hour after its original departure time.

Growing increasingly agitated, she approached the service desk once more. Before she could open her mouth, the woman behind the counter stopped her.

"Ma'am, as I told you the last ten times you asked, the flight *has not* been canceled. At least not yet.

"I assure you, you will be able to board along with the rest of the passengers who are waiting patiently."

Taken aback by the woman's condescending tone, Freya threatened, "I promise your superiors will hear of your rudeness. You know your airline is not the only one flying into New York—"

"And, as I told you the last time, I am more than happy to book you on *any* other flight."

Duly chastised, Freya threw up her hands and returned to her seat, muttering under her breath.

While the letter from Sela had provided an excuse to flee both the city she had, unexpectedly, fallen in love with, and the man who had caused it, Freya wished it could be different. Wished Odin would butt out of her life and let her be happy... for once.

She glanced down the concourse... certain Sean would pop up to stop her from leaving him, despite knowing he could not get past security.

That said, it would not surprise her if the fool bought a ticket just because, which was the reason she had not told him her flight details... or even that their time together had come to an end more quickly than either anticipated.

Freya's heart clenched. The man knew her so well.

He seemed to sense what she was thinking before she did, and had wielded a brand of sorcery, in its own way, as powerful as hers. He had snuck under her defenses, seduced her with his Irish lilt and twinkling green eyes. Revived her and rekindled a flame, she believed doused forever.

Not even Yiannis had managed that.

Freya faded into memories of the past few months with Sean. Of how his devotion had helped her recover from the pain of losing Loki. A pain, she had thought impossible to eradicate. A pain Sean did not know had precipitated her odyssey which ended at the Emerald Isle... and in his arms... his wonderfully strong arms.

She tried to banish the emotions crowding in... with minimal success, it must be admitted

Coincidence, happenstance, or Fate? Freya was in no doubt that Fate had a hand in her change of fortune. Until Odin interfered.

"Flight Nine Eight Five has been cleared to board," announced the harried attendant at the door.

"Perfect timing," Freya growled under her breath. "Introspection gets a person nowhere."

Given she was booked to travel business class, Freya walked the desk where the attendants were checking boarding cards, to find it was, yet again, a case of hurry up and wait. "I'm sorry, Ma'am, but you need to wait for the pre-boards to embark first," the attendant tried to explain.

Freya's temper hanging by a thread, it was a toss-up between evaporating the damn woman and slapping her into next week but, aware she was in full view of a plane load of people, controlled her pique.

In a fitting closure of *this* particular circle, Freya — as she had done with the cabbie when first she arrived in Dublin — nudged the beleaguered woman's mind.

Immediately, the attendant's dismissive attitude transformed and — to the mild confusion of the waiting flight crew — escorted Freya to the business class section as though she was royalty, ensured she was comfortably seated, and arranged for a glass of the best champagne.

After such a trying day, a goddess deserved some respect.

The ominous clouds clung to their rancor as Freya's plane queued for takeoff. Staring through the window, Freya sent a silent petition to her brother, Freyr, "Please, let me get out of here before you release whatever hissy fit you're planning."

Relief coursed through her as the huge metal bird rolled down the runway, gathered speed, and took off into the sky — America bound.

The further west Freya traveled, the more it became evident that Freyr had *no* intention of watching over his sister's flight. The rough air high above the open waters of the North Atlantic, as the plane crossed the point of no return, pitched the great 787 back and forth like a toy being shaken in the hands of an angry child.

No matter how high the jet climbed, it could not clear the billowing mass of clouds.

The heavens opened with a terrible light show. Lightning bolts streaked around the plane, torrents of rain blurred out any visual references.

In the cockpit, the pilots struggled to keep the craft stable, thankful for the banks of instruments.

Freya whispered to her brother, "I appreciate your efforts to slow the flight, but this is going a bit *too* far."

A patch of turbulence so violent the overhead compartment doors burst open — their contents dumped onto the floor and passengers — was his only answer.

Grumbling, Freya threatened, "Just wait until I get my hands on you. I'll show you the real meaning of a tantrum."

The voice of the captain crackled over the intercom. "Ladies and gentlemen, due to extreme weather conditions in New York, and our inability to circumnavigate this storm, we are being diverted to Reagan National in DC.

"I will make another announcement when we begin our descent. Please make yourselves comfortable and keep your seatbelts fastened at all times. Until we clear this turbulence, the cabin crew will not be serving refreshments."

Despite the outwardly unflappable tone of the pilot, Freya registered that even he was nervous about the severity of this storm.

As though the immense choir in the church to which Sean had taken her — insisting it was an experience not to be missed — had launched into a funeral dirge, pleas and prayers to various Gods began to fill Freya's head.

Oddly, she would take the banshee-like tuneless laments to this anytime. Apparently, every single passenger had a sin to confess before their imminent demise... save one.

She discerned her neighbor across the aisle — a portly, red faced, and rather sweaty gentleman — grousing to himself, "Great, I wasted all this money on a business class trip to the Big Apple as a treat for my fiftieth birthday, and now there's a decent probability, I'm about to die sober. Can this flight get any worse?"

Freya could summon her cats to whisk her to safety on a whim but something about this man's simple honesty and understandable vexation touched her soul, sparking a desire to remain seated — safety belt securely fastened, of course — and grant the man several more birthdays.

Damn the Fates, we will *land in one piece.*

Focusing her concentration on the jet, she created a buffer around it, stronger than her brother's storm.

Freyr, who had thought himself more powerful than his sister, beat a hasty retreat when she exerted her authority.

Moments later, the captain provided an update. "We are in contact with Reagan who are doing their best to ensure you make your connections. It appears the storm is lessening to our south more quickly than forecast, and the attendants will be able to serve refreshments shortly."

Freya 'heard' the man's seat squeak as he relaxed, followed by a smug, "I knew they were worrying about nothing. Mind, I'll be demanding comp for my missing lunch."

His remark made her chuckle, which elicited a quizzical glance from her flight companion, who shot her an unrepentant grin and sat back to wait for his birthday bubbly.

The leaden clouds above Washington were scattering. Swathes of blue parted the gray allowing dazzling beams of sunlight to dance across the wet ground.

Freya grinned at the glimmering double rainbow, Freyr had created as an apology for overstepping himself. "Good job I love you," she sent a silent reply. "Don't do it again."

Once the jet came to a halt at the bridgeway, the usual stampede of humanity headed towards the door.

Freya was in no hurry to join them, and waited for the masses to disembark. When the pudgy man stood to gather his carry-ons from the overhead locker, Freya caught his eye.

"I hope the rest of your birthday is better than this flight," she said with a sweet smile.

Without thinking, he replied in a charming brogue, "Aye, as do I. Hopefully my daughter and grandchildren are still—"

Stopping mid-tug on his bag, his disbelieving gaze dropped to the elegant woman waiting patiently for him to finish.

"How did you know it was my birthday?"

Freya's eyes sparkled mischievously. "I overheard the attendant passing on her best wishes when she brought you that last glass of champagne with the extra chocolates."

They shared a laugh.

"Aye, nothing's secret these days, and was very generous, so it was. Well, I must be on my way, dear lady. I hope your travels take you to a happy destination."

"Remains to be seen, but thank you for the thought."

The man nodded and, with a cheerful wave, disappeared through the door.

Alone — with the exception of the flight crew — Freya

stood and stretched. She reached into the overhead locker to retrieve her travel bag, which had slid to the back.

As she contemplated climbing onto the plush seat to recover it, a husky male voice stayed her movement.

"If you hang around here much longer, you're going to miss the connection the airport has organized to get you to New York."

Turning in the direction of the voice, Freya came face to face with one of the smartly uniformed pilots.

Looking him up and down, she replied artlessly, "I've had enough today. I would just as soon find a good meal and a comfortable bed."

Glancing into the compartment the woman was trying to reach, the man spotted a lone bag, which he assumed was her hand luggage. Without being asked, he lifted it down, but refused to hand it over.

"Traveling light, or do you have a matching suitcase in the hold?"

"No. It's just the one. Gives me an excuse to go shopping. Although, had I known the pilot of my flight was resolved to serve as my personal porter, I would have packed more."

"I'm sorry to inform you, ma'am, I am only the copilot. Since, however, I am toting your suitcase, might I suggest a good hotel with an exceptional restaurant? That is, unless you have already made arrangements?" He quirked a questioning brow.

"I was taught to be wary of strange men in uniform, but you look like a trustworthy boy scout."

"Then allow me to take the lead... oh, and fear not... I always come prepared for emergencies."

"I'll keep that in mind."

After spending the evening with her knight in shining armor, dining on gourmet Cornish hens and expensive champagne — something not exactly to her taste, spoiled by Sean's dark draft — Freya felt obliged to invite him up to her room.

The tryst which followed made Freya miss Sean even more. The co-pilot lacked finesse, and was more interested in his pleasure than hers.

Around 2:30, Freya woke him from a deep and noisy sleep.

"Is it morning yet?" he asked drowsily.

"No, but it is time for you to find other accommodation."

Tossing him his discarded uniform, Freya *persuaded* him to dress.

Half-way through, she lost patience. Grabbing him by the arm, she escorted him to the door, sending him away with a kiss on the cheek. She did not even bother to leave him with her usual intoxicating memory.

Slamming the door on the room-less pilot, Freya leaned her head against the cool paneling, angry with herself for being so foolish.

Taking a breath, she wandered over to the window and watched the nightlife of Washington pass beneath her. She had no real interest in it, but the coming and going of strangers filled time before she made the call she had been avoiding since she landed.

Picking up her cellphone from the bedside table, she hit speed dial.

A groggy female voice grumbled on the other end, "Isn't it a little late, sorry early, to be calling?"

"Stop complaining, I'm back in the country, aren't I?"

"Yeah, but I'm guessing you're not calling from the airport."

"No, I'm in DC right now. Flight was diverted. Bad weather."

"Yeah, thank your damn brother for blowing one of our windows in. When do you think you'll arrive?"

"I'm taking the noon train. I should be at Moynihan Train Hall around three-thirty."

"The train? Why not the cat-pack?"

"I've always wanted to take the train and, besides, the cats need their rest as well."

Sela sighed, "It feels like you are trying to avoid us."

Freya forced herself to answer immediately, avoiding the tell-tale pause which would confirm Sela's suspicion.

"Please, just promise to meet me tomorrow."

"Fine... get some sleep," Sela instructed. "I want to hear all about Europe."

The following evening found Freya in the same unpalatable room and board which had driven her from the city in the first place.

This round was more hellish on Freya's heart than the last. The sounds of unbridled passion in the adjoining room made her long for Sean all the more.

FOURTEEN

It had taken the entirety of Freya's absence for Sela to prevail upon Loki to uphold his pledge of undying love.

It was not that Loki regretted proposing, it was more that the concept of marriage as an institution terrified the crap out of him.

Despite his time as a priest in this realm, instructing the church's youth on the values and virtues of marriage, not to mention abstaining from sex until such time as they said their vows — which in hindsight was pure hypocrisy on his part — to swear fealty to one and only one was a pledge, he feared he could not keep.

He was the master of deception.

Is it not inevitable, I'll crush Sela's heart and soul eventually?

If anyone had the fortitude to drag a Norse deity in front of a City Clerk, it was Sela Helsdatter. Something she succeeded in doing after threatening to walk out on him.

The couple waited in the marbled hallway of the New York City's Marriage Bureau for their turn.

Playfully, they nudged each other like nervous teens on their first date.

All of this came under the watchful eye of their sole witness, Freya.

The goddess had not planned to return to this city...*ever*...but Sela could be extremely persuasive when she wanted something — evidenced by the imminent nuptials.

My fault, I suppose, she contended internally. *Had I not intervened in Peer's plans to drag Sela back to the underworld, she would have failed from the start.*

Then, there was Sela's future husband. Freya's heart sank in recollection of the times she had seen Loki at his worst and best through the realms... and in bed.

It was hard for her to stomach their demonstrative behavior. It was almost *too* pure, and made her wonder how much of *their* relationship Loki had divulged to his mate.

Her friendship with Sela, and the mere fact of her presence, inferred he had said nothing.

Her mind drifted to the previous night when Sela and she had yielded to the peculiar tradition indulged in by mortals, the bachelorette party.

The concept continued to baffle her but, she had to admit, it was a fun evening, during which she had given Sela her wedding *gifts*.

Freya believed she had done her friend a favor by bestowing on her some minor magic. Without it, Sela's husband might harm her accidentally, something she had seen happen with the last human he became involved with.

The one thing Freya feared she ought to have left alone was Sela's coin — in Freya's opinion, an ugly, hateful thing. She had charmed it into a talisman, which now hung on a chain around Sela's neck.

When she touched the metal, Freya had sensed a

burgeoning power, unable to discern whether it radiated directly from the coin, or was a lingering echo of Peer's influence, or...

Studying Sela as the couple's number was called, for the briefest instant, Freya swore she saw a shimmer in her friend's aura.

Her eyes widened when she discerned it again as the trio stood before the registrar to recite the state's wedding vows.

For the love of Nature... no... please do not let it be true.

The man finished up with the standard, "You may kiss the bride."

Sela and Loki cemented their vows in a kiss so passionate, Freya deemed it pertinent to separate them before they consummated the marriage there and then.

Lost in the heady moment, Sela's cheeks flared a deep rose, but she could not contain her joy, and drew her best friend into an ecstatic hug.

The jolt which hit Freya, nearly knocked her off her feet.

Her face a contorted mask, she took a step back and gaped at Sela in disbelief.

Confused by Freya's reaction, Sela tried to assess what was wrong with the goddess.

"F-Freya... what is it?"

Freya lifted a trembling hand to cover her gawking mouth. In a burst of jealous temper, she hissed, "H-how could you?"

"What? Freya, for Odin's sake, what's wrong?"

"Y-You're with child." Tears streamed down Freya's face, thinking of the number of times Loki had gifted her with life only to have it snatched from her before it could develop.

"No, Freya, you're mista—"

"Liar. Is *this* why you are forcing him to marry you?"

Putting a distance between them, Freya gave the pair a dark look, not sure what else to say.

Then, as though being chased by a horde of enraged valkyries, fled.

Freya sought refuge at the Four Seasons Hotel where she pondered her next move. Her only venture out was to the hotel bar where she attempted to drown her sorrows.

A complete waste of time, given it would take almost the entire stock of spirits to dull her over-reaction to perceiving Sela's pregnancy.

"Of course, she would be," Freya scoffed to the bartender. "The two of them copulate like monkeys in heat, b-but why couldn't it be me..." overcome by another bout of sobs.

Downing the last of her drink, she retreated to her room.

Slamming the door to her suite, Freya leaned against it, pulled herself together, mopped her tears, and closed her eyes.

Mentally, she spun the wheel in search of a new place, she could escape to. Europe had proved fruitless for her... and had been even more traumatic to her psyche than returning to New York had.

There nothing left for her here and, she was becoming more and more convinced, there was nowhere in this realm to soothe the ache in her soul, or fill the vacuum in her heart.

Without bothering to check out, or pay her bill, Freya threw her future to the Fates, vanishing from the city she once loved, and now despised.

CHAPTER
FIFTEEN

ven for a Friday night, the casino was unusually busy. The storms of the past couple of nights had canceled the local high school football games and had chased most of the locals in for something to do.

Dasan Blackwolf was always happiest when it thundered because, inevitably, bad weather led to the farmers and ranchers scuttling in with their pockets stuffed full of cash.

Currently, he was monitoring the security screens from his office, and musing inwardly, *a good night for a front row seat from where I can watch these idiots blow any money they just earned, selling their livestock at market.*

Unbeknownst to his gullible clientele, Dasan was also a silent-majority partner in the local stockyards. A crooked operator in every facet of his life, business or pleasure who, unapologetically, screwed the ranchers out of what little profit they made at every corner and turn.

You didn't get to where he was by feeling sorry for people. He didn't force them into the casino and, if the punters didn't realise the house never lost, that was not his problem.

Dasan's levity came to an abrupt halt when he saw his Pit Boss, William Fighting Bear, flagging the camera and trying to fiddle with his earpiece near one of the High Roller Blackjack tables.

Registering how flustered his Number One was becoming, Dasan contemplated whether the night was about to go pear-shaped.

Heaving a frustrated sigh, he made his way down from the office.

As he crossed the casino floor, he was stopped by a couple of regulars. He paused to greet them for appearances' sake, but his eyes remained fixed on the table next to William and the growing crowd congregating around it.

He flashed a trained smile to the couple, promised them complimentary tickets for dinner, and excused himself.

Reaching the table, Dasan hooked William by the arm and, casually, escorted the worried Pit Boss to one side. Making sure he could observe the table, Dasan asked the question, William did *not* want to answer.

"What the hell is going on?"

William glanced over his shoulder. "She's been playing for the last two hours and winning... big."

Outwardly calm, Dasan said, "Have you switched out the dealer yet?"

"Yeah, we switched in the third new dealer about an hour ago. What do you suggest? Security is onto her, but they cannot decode her system. It's impossible to count eight decks continually, which is what she must be doing. We have no clue how she keeps winning. You know how we run the tables."

"Counting that many decks is easier than you think,

Bill. My six-year-old can manage five, but if security hasn't caught her out, I doubt she's doing that. Stay vigilant, we can't afford to lose *too* much."

Spotting beads of perspiration appearing on his dealer's brow, Dasan added, "Send Buck on a break before he has a heart attack. Replace him with Rachel. If anyone can put an end to this woman's streak, sit's Rachel.

"Also, get the little lady set up as a VIP."

Dasan scoured the floor for his favorite Executive Host, but there was no sign of her.

"Find Molly. If she isn't free, *see that she is*. I want her to do what she does best, and make sure she does not leave the woman's elbow. After a few complimentary drinks, things are sure to settle down."

Leaving William to issue his orders, Dasan headed upstairs to have a conversation with the guys in the Security Booth.

Swiping his keycard over the lock, he entered the dimly lit room and made himself comfortable next to his Security Chief, Matt Holsten.

"Your peeps have any idea what scam the woman on table two is running?" Dasan watched the dealers being switched out.

He noted the woman looked a little annoyed at the interruption to the game, but didn't speak to either dealer as they swapped places.

His brow shot up to his hairline when the woman tossed Buck a fifty-dollar chip.

Matt saw the tip as well, but was more annoyed at Dasan calling his Security Detail *Peeps*.

"We only spy on the players cuz we have to, Dasan," Matt spat without taking his eyes off the screen, "and don't get excited about the tip. So far, she's given every dealer the same."

"Thoughts on her scheme?" Dasan asked.

"Whatever it is, I wished she'd teach me. I've never seen anything like it. She lost her first couple of hands, but hasn't since. It's like she knows the dealer's card before it's flipped."

"You saying she's psychic? Should we ask her to wear an aluminum hat?" Dasan sniped.

"Just telling ya what I see."

At the table, the woman watched the new dealer shuffle the multiple decks with the flourish of a magician. Bored with the dexterous display, she twisted in her chair, hoping to flag down a passing cocktail waitress.

She saw a dark, slender woman approaching the table, smiling politely.

"That's true magic." The woman returned the smile. "Someone here can read my mind. How novel is that?"

Hiding her confusion at the remark, the waitress introduced herself, "Hi, I'm Molly. What can I get you, on the House?"

"Since I doubt this place has mead, how about a gin and tonic," the woman replied.

"My pleasure, ma'am," Molly said genially, glancing at Rachel to see whether she had managed to figure out their guest.

Rachel gave an almost imperceptible shake of her head as she filled the Blackjack shoe with the cards.

The woman noted the subtle exchange, but said nothing, toying with the growing stack of chips in front of her.

Molly returned with the double-strength cocktail, and loitered near the woman's chair now responsible for ensuring the glass was never empty, aware the brass upstairs were watching.

Rachel waited until Molly placed the drink by the woman's elbow before she started to deal, hoping the bar had *not* skimped on the gin, as per the norm. She wanted to win back the House's money quickly and go home.

The overtime is nice, but a warm bed with Teddy beats it any night.

As the night progressed, not even Rachel was able to throw the woman off her game. Her winning continued and, fueled with alcohol, her bets were becoming increasingly large.

At about 1 a.m., Rachel changed the decks yet again and dealt the woman a hand with the Ace of Hearts showing. Rachel cursed to herself because she was sure she had fixed the deck and it was impossible for the ace to slip through, but there it was.

Transfixed by the woman's smile, as the down card was flipped to show the Ace of Diamonds, Rachel shot a look up to the camera, questioning her next move.

"Shit," was the word murmured by the management.

The woman peeled her gaze from the dealer to the camera overhead and winked at it, saying, "Good thing we aren't playing poker. It would be a waste having these two as a measly pair."

Re-focusing on the dealer, she grinned. "Let's split the pair, love."

Hiding a yawn, she checked her watch. "I'm tired. I reckon this will be my last hand of the night. Let's make it interesting."

The woman picked up a pile of chips from her winnings — matching what she had already placed on the first ace — to stack them, neatly, on the newly turned ace.

Folding her hands on the table, she waited patiently for the next two cards to be dealt...

They never appeared.

Instead, a large hand, adorned with a heavy silver and turquoise ring, land on her shoulder.

The woman studied the fingers, determining they had never done an honest day's work in their entire life.

Her eyes tracked up the arm, the hand was connected to, and she stifled a chuckle when she saw a rather haggard looking gentleman, looming over her. His suit was wrinkled and disheveled as a result of its owner hunching over a monitor trying to catch her doing something suspicious.

She quirked her finely shaped brow at the man, whom she assumed to be the casino manager, and asked innocently, "Is there a problem, sir."

Maintaining his composure in front of the crowd of locals who had refused to leave the table, he replied, "I'm afraid the casino is not able to cover a bet that large, ma'am but, if you come with me, we will settle your current winnings."

Dasan crooked his elbow, and directed Security to collect her chips. His expression indicated he was not about to take *no* for an answer.

The woman shrugged, picked up her drink, and extracted a chip from the stack.

Rather than flicking the tip to Rachel, as she had done with the previous dealers, she leaned over and pressed it into Rachel's palm.

With a low chuckle, she advised, "You need more practice at being inconspicuous when you stack a deck."

The woman's caution, and accompanying awareness that she knew what was afoot yet remained amicable, made Rachel blush.

She opened her hand to find a hundred-dollar chip tucked in it, making her feel worse.

Shoving the tip in her apron pocket, Rachel reached over the table to collect the cards. Her hand froze when she saw, in place of the two Aces, face up awaiting their next cards, lay a seven of Diamonds and a six of Hearts.

Rachel's eyes shot to the woman who was being led out by her boss.

Hooking her hand around Dasan's waiting arm, the woman matched his pace as they crossed the casino floor, and past the Cages, wholly aware she was being escorted out of the casino minus any of her winnings.

"You know I might have lost that last hand."

Dasan shook his head. "No, somehow I doubt that was going to happen."

They stopped at the door, the rain still pelting the glass. Dasan disentangled his arm from the woman's grasp and bade her a good evening, warning, "You will not be permitted entry in this casino, or any on the Reservation."

Freya watched the rain for a few seconds. "That's a shame. You had such attentive staff. I don't suppose you'd offer a girl a ride home, would you?"

Dasan spun on his heel, leaving her to face the storm.

No sooner had he reached the casino floor, than he got a squeal through his earpiece.

"This is Matt. Surveillance just picked up that crazy

bitch from the Blackjack table stealing one of the casino's pickups."

"How the hell? I just left her—"

The Head Teller from the Cage cut in mid-sentence, "Dasan, what kinda shit are you pulling?"

"What the fuck are you talking about, Henry?"

"I've got two neatly stacked trays of chips from Blackjack, but none of the girls remember paying out a hundred thousand in winnings to anybody tonight. Are you authorizing payouts without the VP's consent? The Council will have your ass—"

Dasan yelled into the earpiece, "Get off the line, Henry. Matt get the Tribal Police out here. *Now*."

Freya cursed her brother, "You can shut off the damn water works anytime you fancy, Freyr."

Which seemed to have the opposite effect.

She wound down the window far enough to shove her middle finger skyward. He should have no problem seeing it; the weather was his responsibility and this storm bore all the hallmarks of his handiwork.

The gust of wind that hit the truck broadside, made her seize the wheel, fighting to keep the truck in the correct lane.

"Where's a good cat-drawn chariot when you need one?" Freya muttered balefully.

SIXTEEN

The blare of sirens seemed to be surrounding her.

Unsure exactly where she was on US 212 — her vision hampered by sheets of rain — Freya knew she had to get off the Reservation before anybody caught her.

Blindly, she drove west as fast as she could.

Glancing at the bag of neatly bundled 'winnings' on the seat next to her, Freya shook her head. Occasionally, and usually when she was under stress, her ego overruled her common sense, resulting in acts of reckless stupidity. Tonight's antics could be classified as her most crack-brained to date.

If she so chose, Freya could conjure up the entire US mint, although she surmised the United States Government might notice if their Denver Mint went missing, but was proud of making it this far without incident, *or magic*.

None of that mattered now, because she was lost on a rainy country road somewhere in the state of Montana, with no idea what she was doing.

"That gut-griping clotpole of a Casino Manager. He just

had to say no, didn't he? When will humans learn *not* to challenge me!"

She did not need the cash, she was a Norse Goddess, in fact, she was *the* Goddess. Fólkvangr was hers, this world was hers — maybe therein lay the problem.

Having everything at one's fingertips, leads to boredom, she mused.

Which, inevitably, prompted her to behave rashly.

Boredom tainted the clarity of her judgment, made her crave being a victim time and again just to get attention.

To make Odin remember he is supposed to be married to me... or stir Loki's interest...

Loki.

Freya's heart ached as memories crowded in. He had been hers at a whim; simultaneously, protector and adversary. How could she not love him?

Those days were gone.

He belonged to another.

Someone who had opened her heart to him, who loved him unconditionally. Something Freya was unable to do.

"Why did you not rot in Niflheim, Sela Helsdatter," she fumed.

A flash of lightning dazzled her.

The jarring stop, accompanied by the crunch of metal, informed Freya, she had missed the onramp to Interstate 90.

That she was watching the storm through the passenger side window confirmed she was on her side and the truck was done for.

"Are you happy now, Freyr?" she sniped at the deluge. A stray thunderclap mocked her in response.

Struggling to climb out of the overturned vehicle, Freya vowed her undying antipathy to the repugnant imbeciles in Valhalla, and that she would *never* use magic again.

As usual, it had led her into trouble.

And, as usual, she had followed along without heed or care.

This time, Freya refused to let the Fates' temptations hold her captive. She promised to extricate herself from their hold with intelligence and cunning — not cheap parlor tricks.

Jumping down onto the muddy ground, the sodden land squished under her boots. She stood next to the truck, trying to get her bearings.

In the distance, she spied a set of headlights. "I cannot catch a damn break." Impotently, she kicked the tire, certain this was the law.

The lights drew closer. She registered there were no blue lights and no sirens.

Perhaps my luck is changing?

An old pickup crawled along the verge to where Freya had skidded off the road, and came to a halt, engine idling.

Confused, and concerned, Freya waited. No one had exited the truck. "Hello?" she ventured, hesitantly.

A tall, lone figure slid out of the cab, and stood in front of the lights.

Freya could see it was a man, his hand planted firmly on his hat to prevent it blowing away. The collar of his jacket was turned up in an, unsuccessful, attempt to keep the rest of him dry.

"Looks like ya missed the turn," Freya's would be rescuer observed.

Master of the understatement, Freya thought to herself, saying brightly, "Yeah, storm spooked a deer and when I swerved to miss it..." she swung one arm out encompassing the mangled wreck.

"With all the Deer Crossing signs this state has, you'd figure the deer would have developed the smarts to know where to go by now. You hurt?"

"No, just a little shaken. Where you heading?"

"Hopefully, Billings before I call it a night. I can give ya a ride into Crow Agency if you want, where you can get ahold of the Tribal Cops to report the accident."

"Fuck, I'm still on Reservation Land?" Freya spoke more loudly than she intended.

"There a problem with that?" the figure inquired.

Ignoring the question and scrambling up the embankment, Freya asked, "Any chance of hitching a lift to Billings instead?"

"Don't know why you'd want to go there. Next town is just a few miles ahead, and—"

Freya summoned up her best desperate 'damsel-in-distress' expression, ably assisted by the rain because it was impossible to tell whether her *tears* were genuine.

"Please, sir, I'd be very grateful if you could take me to Billings. I'll even pay for the gas once we get there."

The man's gaze shifted between her and the overturned truck.

There was an interesting story behind the mangled vehicle and the drenched woman who had somehow survived apparently unscathed.

Besides, he was not a fan of the Tribal Police, even if

some were kin. He'd had enough run-ins driving through here.

Their treatment of Non-Res people left a sour taste in his mouth, especially after witnessing shake downs of unwary travelers.

"Just to Billings?" his resolve weakening.

"And no farther," Freya promised... unless she could work her legendary charms and change his mind between here and there.

By the time the pair passed Crow Agency, the rain had stopped. The curtain of thick clouds, which had dominated the sky, parted slowly to reveal the vast expanse of a crystal-clear Montana night.

Freya was not quite sure what her brother was up to but, as long as she was in a warm truck driving away from her current problems, she did not care.

She glanced at the man who hadn't spoken since he had held the door open for her to climb inside the truck. The dash lights illuminated his face. He was not a particularly attractive male — although, to be fair, her benchmark included Gods — but there was something captivating about his rugged features, the weathered cragginess of his face.

"Thank you for rescuing me tonight," Freya offered a tentative smile.

"Don't usually pick up women along the road," his voice reminiscent of gravel grinding, "but I was raised to help where I could."

He paused. "The name's Jacob, by the way. Figure if

we're gonna be traveling together, I ought to introduce myself."

Freya was surprised he had taken the initiative. He didn't appear the type to comply with customs or traditions, or manners for that matter.

"My name is..." Freya vacillated. Introducing herself as a Norse Goddess would, undoubtedly result in being dumped at the nearest mental hospital, post haste, if not being kicked out of this comfortable truck with dispatch.

"You forget your name? You sure you didn't hit your head in the crash and end up with amnesia or something?" Jacob prodded, a hint of concern in his question.

Freya laughed softly, "No, Jacob, I remember my name just fine. It's Freda... Freda Odinson." hating the sound of the name as soon as she said it.

Why on earth did I choose that name?

Too late, she was stuck with it now, and what did it matter? Their relationship would be over before he knew how to spell it.

Her traveling companion tried it on for size. "Well, Freda Odinson, I'm guessing you're not from around here. So, who do you plan to call once we reach Billings?"

"What makes ya think that I'm not a local. You don't know everybody in Montana," Freya defended herself.

"That accent of yours says otherwise. I'm figuring you for a New Yorker, it's not annoying enough for Boston."

"What do you know of either city?"

Jacob shrugged off the implied slight. "We get satellite out here."

The conversation lapsed into silence from that point. Neither knew the other well enough to launch into the typical friend-to-friend banter of road trips.

Watching the night roll by, Freya decided to bide her

time, using it to consider her next move. It was becoming evident, Billings was the end of the line for her.

The assumption triggered the return of the gnawing feeling of hopelessness in the pit of her stomach, which had plagued her throughout Europe.

Oh, Sean, what are you up to tonight?

Not even the memory of her Irish lover was able to mask the loneliness caused by the loss of the god she truly missed.

The answer as to *what he was up to* was not hard to surmise.

Damn you, Sela. Freya fought the tears brimming in her drowsy eyes. The gentle rocking of the truck gave her no more time for self-pity, as sleep overtook her.

Jacob cruised into the service station outside Billings. Coming to a stop at the gas pumps, he looked over at his passenger. Even under the harsh glare of the fluorescent lights, he was captivated by her beauty.

It amazed him that her face gave no clue to her age. When he first came upon her, he pegged her for being in her twenties, but her language told him she was older... much older... than he originally believed.

He reached for the door handle, deciding to not wake her *quite* yet. She looked as though she could use the extra shut-eye before the two went their separate ways.

The squeak of the pickup's door and the overhead cab light as Jacob climbed out, put paid to his thoughtful sentiment.

Blinking, Freya rubbed her eyes, and stretched,

swearing she had been asleep for days instead of a mere forty-five minutes.

She glanced at the driver's seat to ask Jacob where they were, to see it was vacant. Befuddled from sleeping so deeply, she wondered what had happened to her chauffeur, and alighted from the truck, to spot him pumping gas.

In a manner at odds with her refined and ladylike appearance, once her feet hit the ground, she yawned and scratched herself with both hands like a Norse fisherman.

"We in Billings yet?" She could not prevent a second yawn.

"Yeah, just outside."

"Oh, okay," Freya said matter-of-factly. "I guess I'll get my stuff and head out to find a…" she paused mid-sentence, noticing Jacob was staring at her oddly.

"What's wrong?" She frowned.

The lack-luster blue of her eyes told Jacob there was more to this Freda Odinson's troubled life than a wrecked stolen truck on the reservation. It was also blatantly clear that whoever she *planned* to call would not be in a position to rescue her from the Montana night.

If, in fact, there *was* anyone to call.

Putting the nozzle back into the pump, he skirted around her to the open passenger door. Hand on the metal frame, he said, "Hop in."

Hesitantly, Freya scanned the forecourt. Uncertain of his motives — *was this a kidnapping attempt?* — to extinguish him among the gas pumps would, inevitably, result in collateral damage… and probably several more deaths.

Her equivocation made Jacob chuckle.

"Don't worry, my grandmother would come down from the heavens and kick my ass if I even thought about doing anything untoward.

"I'm hungry," he went on, "and could use a dining companion. You game?"

Relief coursed through her, but she hid it behind a shy smile, and accepted his invitation. Climbing back into the passenger seat, she warned, "I have a healthy appetite... and a vicious left if you try anything."

Before he shut the door, he quipped, "I have no doubt of either."

By the time dawn peeked over the edge of the Montana sky, the two had overcome the verbal awkwardness.

While a trifle leery of each other, they had managed to drain numerous cups of coffee and learned the disasters of the other's love life.

Although Freya had chosen to withhold any pertinent names, she had bared her heart to Jacob, finding him unusually attentive to her plight. She was fortunate to find a man willing to listen and share, so soon after losing Se... she pushed that thought away. *Not the time, Freya, not the time.*

Not even Loki had been this honest, Freya bit back the urge to laugh at the irony, *with me.*

Jacob's coffee cup settling in its matching saucer interrupted Freya's thoughts.

Out of nowhere, he declared, "Look, Freda, I feel bad leaving you stranded here waiting until a decent hour before you can make that call. How about coming back to the ranch and calling from there. At least you'd be more comfortable."

He pulled his buck knife from its sheath and slid it across the table.

"Hold onto it, might ease whatever terrible thoughts you harbor about my intentions."

Lifting the blade, Freya studied the intricate scrimshaw on the deer bone handle. She had not seen such craftsmanship since her days in the Norse forests.

Tucking it into her bag, Freya reassured Jacob, "Trust me, I have more dangerous weapons with which to defend myself... although I shall consider your knife to be a cherished gift, you're never getting back."

As they shared a laugh and prepared to leave the truck stop, Freda Odinson was born.

nlike the drive to Billings, which had been blessedly silent, the trip to Wise River proved anything but peaceful.

Once Jacob had unlocked Freya's mouth, he could not get her to shut up. The speed with which she rattled off one story after another made his head spin, and threatened to transcend into a migraine.

She touched on her life in New York, conveniently excluding any names of people Jacob might be inclined to contact, in order to find someone to claim her.

She described her adventures, traveling through Europe, in vivid detail, including her newfound fascination with Guinness... a beer he found repugnant... thanks to some Irish bartender.

If she plans on sticking around... she'd better learn to appreciate decent American beer, Jacob ruminated, the iconic blue ribbon logo of Pabst popping into his head.

No Irish horse piss in my house.

Unknowingly pressing the accelerator closer to the floor of the old truck, Jacob did not realize he was cruising at close to ninety until a Montana state trooper popped up behind him outside Bozeman.

Spotting the flashing lights in her side mirror, Freya fell silent, tugging her coat closer around her face in hopes of concealing herself.

Jacob, his ears noting their reprieve, glanced at the woman next to him, then at the patrol car looming larger in his rearview mirror by the second.

A check of his speedometer foretold the trouble he was in. Coming to a halt at the side of the road, he watched the state trooper pull in behind him.

Before the man made it to his window, Jacob had his license and registration at the ready. This was not the first time he had been stopped; it tended to be a bit of an occupational hazard for any Native American.

Tapping his flashlight on Jacob's window, the trooper instructed, "License and registration please."

Taking Jacob's proffered papers, the officer studied them with his flashlight.

Tilting his light back toward Jacob, he asked the standard question, "Do you know why I pulled you over?"

"Yes, officer, my foot got the better of me. I didn't realize how fast I was driving."

"You do know, I can have you arrested, and your truck impounded for reckless driving?"

"I do, sir, but I hope you won't. My lady friend over there..."

The trooper stopped Jacob mid-sentence, turning his light on Freya. Studying her for a moment, he became concerned she was not moving.

"Ma'am, can I see your ID as well?"

Freya did not respond.

"Ma'am," the trooper tried once more, "I need you to sit up and face me. I need to make sure you're okay."

An angry voice grumbled, "Dammit, Jacob, I told you to turn the radio down... my head still hurts and I need sleep."

Jacob looked at the trooper, and gave an apologetic shrug.

"As you can see, she doesn't travel well. Took something a while back to knock her out for the drive, but I guess it hasn't kicked in.

"Kinda the reason I was speeding... wanted to get her home before the devil unleashes from her."

Flashing his light between the two again, the trooper stepped back from the truck, and made his way to his patrol car. He climbed in and radioed the dispatcher for any warrants on the driver and vehicle.

While the trooper was busy running his checks... a conversation was being carried on in the cab of the truck.

"It would be helpful if you didn't just sit there like some corpse, I'm trying to dispose of."

"I don't know, you seem to have done an adequate job weaving a stupid story for him."

Freya realized she was enjoying the banter with Jacob. Even though he had gone out of his way to shelter her from both the weather and the police, he still had the intestinal fortitude to challenge her.

"When he comes back, please have the common decency to assure him, I didn't kidnap you."

"Hell, you keep saying kidnap... how can I be certain you—"

Tap, Tap, Tap

The lens of the patrolman's flashlight rapping on Jacob's window, prompted Freya to change her tune.

Jacob rolled the window down, just in time for the

trooper to hear the formerly taciturn woman in the passenger seat launch into a tirade directed at the driver.

"I told you, I didn't want to go fishing in goddamned Spearfish this weekend, but would you listen? Hell, no!"

The trooper noted the fishing rods resting in the rifle rack attached to the truck's back window.

"Momma warned me about chauvinists like you. Put a fishing rod in your hand and it might as well be your penis. You don't listen when that's in your hand, either."

"Freda. Enough." Jacob barked.

Shaking his head at the bickering couple, for some reason the trooper felt sorry for the man receiving the verbal barrage.

"Look, sir. Promise to keep it under seventy-five, and I'll let you off with a warning."

Freya took a final shot for good measure, "It would serve him right to have you drag his sorry ass to jail for forcing me to travel eight hours to drown worms... not to mention me. I told him it was supposed to pour down."

"Have a pleasant evening," the trooper said with no hint of irony, as he beat a hasty retreat to his car, thankful he was not the one facing the wrath of the formerly sleeping bear.

Jacob waved to the departing vehicle, and then turned to Freya.

An angelic smile spread across her face.

"Was that really necessary?"

"Well, you were the one complaining about my lack of participation. Besides, you should be thanking me. I got you out of the speeding ticket."

"Yeah, and almost landed me in jail for murdering innocent worms. I'm surprised he didn't ask to see my fishing license.

"Fishing licenses? You can drive fish out here?"

"Wait... what?"

"Why else would you need a license for a fish?"

Jacob could not tell whether she was serious. Instead of exploring the conversation further, he shifted the truck into gear and spun the wheels as he regained the highway.

For the remainder of the trip, Freya was glued to her window in tranquil fascination. As they sped by, she was captivated by the quaint houses littering the side of the highway.

She spotted families enjoying a morning's fishing along the river, as well as large herds of cattle grazing on grasses which quivered and swayed under searching noses.

The boundless Montana landscape, reminded Freya of the untamed wilderness of her childhood.

Her eyes widened when Jacob slowed to turn onto a gravel road.

"Are we really going fishing?" she quizzed.

Jacob shook his head, his eyes fixed on the track. "No, I don't have any room in the freezer."

His refusal brought a pout to Freya's radiant face.

"Though," he cast an eye to the river as they crossed a small bridge, "it is full of delicious trout."

"What? Oh,, do you have Fjord Trout here as well?"

"Can't say I've ever seen any of those, but you might like the rainbows."

"Please promise to take me fishing and show me?" Freya asked eagerly.

"We'll see," was Jacob's less than enthusiastic pledge.

As the truck rumbled along, Freya reached out to jerk

the sleeve of Jacob's flannel shirt, almost causing him to serve into the ditch before he could bring the truck to a halt.

Forgetting herself, she squealed, "What in the name of Thor's goats are those shaggy beasts?"

Jacob saw her wagging her finger at a herd of buffalo.

Alighting, he walked around her side of the pickup, to open her door. Taking her by the hand, he led her to the fence line, and although inclined to press her about her strange exclamation, thought better of it.

"Don't tell me yer've never seen buffalo before?"

"Buffalo? Are they friendly? They look like something created by Hel."

"Can't say they are from Hell," Jacob joked, unaware Freya meant a demigod and not a place. "But they can be nasty if treated wrong.

"The plains used to be thick with them. My ancestors said you could walk from the Dakotas to the Rockies across their backs and never touch the ground.

"Our relationship, if you will, with the mighty creatures was symbiotic. We tended to the herds and, in return, they provided food and shelter for us."

He sighed, "Then white man came and slaughtered them almost to extinction for the sake of their farms and railroads."

Freya turned her head to look at Jacob who had grown silent.

He caught her gaze.

"Anyway, I manage this herd for the state. Makes me feel like I'm saving something for future generations."

"Very admirable, sir."

"Okay... we nearly there, ready?"

"Absolutely."

The sight of the extensive log structure looming at the end of the road prompted Freya's, "You live in an inn?"

Jacob chuckled. "No, it's the homestead."

Freya was sure with a place this large, it had to be teeming with people.

"A-Are you married? Why did you drag me all the way out here just to—"

"Hold on, Ms. Odinson, I didn't *drag* you anywhere... and why would I do so if I had a wife?"

"How would I know what kind of perverted games you are planning... but I can assure you, I will not be part of a threesome."

"So, if I prove I'm single... you'll consider sleeping with me? Which of us is the perverted one?"

That comment earned him a punch, usually reserved for Loki, in the arm.

Rubbing his abused limb, he smiled at her.

"I promise there is no Mrs. Lewdly Dressed inside waiting to pounce on you. It's just us.

"Now, if you don't mind, I could use some coffee. It's been a long night, and I guess you have a call to make."

Freya watched him climb down from the truck and walk to the front door. He unlocked and opened it wide, standing on the threshold waiting.

Seeing no one bolting to welcome him home, she followed suit.

As the door shut behind them, Jacob said, "You'll find the phone on the desk. I'll be in the kitchen when you're done."

Alone in the room, Freya crossed to the phone and

picked up the receiver. As she listened to the dial tone, she remembered Odin's cynical farewell.

You will be begging to return.

No... she was on her own and needed to rely on herself and no one else.

Replacing the handset on the cradle, she called after Jacob, "Please will you pour me some coffee, too, and tell me more about buffalos."

CHAPTER
EIGHTEEN

B y the end of the first week, Freya had made herself at home.

Between dodging Jacob's oft repeated, "Did you make your call today?" and, "When are they coming to get you?" Freya appropriated the largest guest room, and had produced blueprints for Jacob to *approve* so she could redecorate it to suit her own tastes.

As if that was not bold enough, she had also explored the outbuildings nestled within the compound.

Over tomahawk steaks, Jacob had prepared on the patio barbeque, Freya laid out her plans to convert the ranch's ancient icehouse into a she-shed... something she had seen on television.

"Hey, my great grandpa built that. I don't think he'd like to see it turned into some fru-fru hideaway."

"It's just sitting there, abandoned, but, fine..." she threw up her hands. "If you think he would be happy seeing all his hard work fall to wrack and ruin..." Freya let that dangle as she stabbed a piece of perfectly cooked medium steak.

"Okay, okay," Jacob relented. "Just keep the cost down,

will you? I'm still trying to figure out how you talked me into remodeling the bedroom... or how I'm gonna pay for it."

Freya studied him. Clearly the decrepit building held some curious sentimental value, and she did not want to upset him... well, not too much... she liked it here. Another possibility insinuated itself into her shrewd brain.

"Instead of refurbishing your precious icehouse, may I propose an alternative?"

"If you're talking about my ranch, the bank still owns the lion's share of it from the mortgage, I had to take out to pay for the livestock."

"No, nothing that drastic. That stable block down the hill, the one with the prettiest white mare... who looks sad and lonely, by the way... what if you were to let me ride her?"

Freya's switch from renovations to riding, came right out of left field, but Jacob was getting used to her convoluted trains of thought.

That said, this request required reining in; the horse in question refused to be broken. He attempted to deflect her, knowing before he spoke that it was futile.

"God, no. Not that one. The hands call her Ball Breaker because she bucks like a sailboat adrift in a storm. You should stay away from her. Last thing I want to explain to a doctor is how I could be so careless as to allow a city girl to get thrown."

"I'll have you know, mister, I know my way around horses, even temperamental ones." Freya's eyes narrowed. "How about this... if she will not let me approach her, I'll respect your wishes."

"Can I hold you to your word?" Jacob needed to hear her promise.

Leaping to her feet, she raced from the stone patio to the stable, replying over her shoulder, "Have I lied to you yet? Never mind...let's just go with yes."

Not trusting his newfound house guest, Jacob jumped up and chased after her.

Jacob beat Freya to the corral's gate by a mere two steps. Throwing himself in front of it before she could swing it open, he made her reiterate her pledge.

"If she so much as bucks, you promise to back off and forget about her."

"Yeah, yeah, Grandpa. Goodness, but you're a killjoy. Now, please step aside and allow *me* to teach *you* a thing or two about horses.

Jacob had no idea, this *city girl* had been taught to ride by Yggdrasil's greatest horseman. Despite his many flaws... too numerous for Freya to count... she could not deny Odin's equine expertise.

In their youth, he had bestowed on Freya his vast knowledge, in hopes of wooing her and — even after she had become an accomplished rider — never failed to tease her about preferring her damn cats to pull her carriage over one of his steeds.

Her answer was always the same, "Horses are too majestic to be yoked to a cart. They are meant to run free. Oh, and unlike horses, it takes a special skill to herd cats... you should try it sometime."

Edging around Jacob, Freya crossed the muddy pen to the stable door, opening it carefully so as not to startle any of the inhabitants.

She took a deep breath. The warm smell of fresh hay and animals at rest reminded her of better times.

Spying a bucket of carrots conveniently placed near the entrance, Freya picked it up and wandered down the hay strewn aisle.

Stopping at each stall, she offered its occupant a carrot. If it was accepted...generally the case...she rubbed the velvety nose and whispered a few nonsense words, receiving a welcoming nicker in return.

Freya reached the last stall, noting the troubled white mare's wary stance, the way she pawed at the back of her enclosure, set for a confrontation with yet another inter-fering human.

The striking creature eyed Freya balefully. She had spent much of her life being tormented by these dratted humans and was weary of it.

Can they not leave me alone?

When the stranger stood at the gate, the mare's ears flattened and she tossed her head in warning, adding a few snorts for good measure.

The newcomer's scent hit the mare's muzzle. There was something different about the woman's essence. It was not human at all, it was heady and inviting, persuading her not to panic... to trust.

The mare saw the carrot and heard the female speaking to her quietly. While the words meant nothing, the tone encouraged the mare to move closer.

Hesitant, at first, the combination of the carrot and this strange being proved irresistible and, before the mare realized, she was at the gate, nibbling on the crunchy vegetable and having her muzzle stroked.

"I know how you feel," the woman murmured. "Neither of us is understood, are we?"

The mare tossed her head and nickered in agreement. She pushed her nose against the female's palm, her ears drooping as she relaxed.

"Do you want to get out of this stall?"

The mare's ears stiffened and her eyes rolled in fear.

The female seemed unaffected, reassuring the mare, calmly, "Easy, girl. I just want to take you for a walk around the corral. Will you allow me?"

Nobody had ever asked the mare for her permission to do anything, and the question took her by surprise. She had done such a good job of frightening everybody off, she never expected to feel the wind in her mane again.

She bobbed her head in tacit agreement, and awaited the dreaded bridle and crop.

"No, little one," the female said, though her lips never moved, "we are not ready for that yet. Let's get you out and run free for a bit. Might you grant me the honor of watching?"

Once more the white mare nodded, and the female opened the gate to lead her out.

For a moment, the mare considered trampling the female under her hooves and fleeing this prison, but the latter's unruffled faith convinced her otherwise.

When they reached the door, the mare halted. She was afraid to step out, afraid this was a trick, exacerbated by the sight of the male at the gate. A sniff confirmed *this* one was human.

The mare started to retreat, threatening to rear up and

bolt, but the reassuring hand on her neck caught her off guard.

As though reading the mare's thoughts, the female soothed, "It's okay, girl, he's a friend. He may look scary but he's as gentle as a colt."

The scent surrounded the mare again, coaxing her to believe. She stepped out into the corral, testing the ground beneath her hooves. Without further encouragement, the mare circled the ring.

Each lap was faster than the last. Her nostrils sucked the sweet fragrance of the recent rain into her lungs. It felt as if she were running across the valley... free.

Spying the female sitting atop the fence...the male leaning on the other side...the mare turned and charged.

She saw the male straighten up, readying for a confrontation but, save one hand lifting, palm out, the female remained motionless.

With scant time to avoid colliding with the fence, the mare heard a soft *whoa* breeze by her ear.

Her hooves dug into the mud, bringing her to a standstill close enough for the female to stretch across and pat her shoulder.

The two had connected, and the equine version of delight suffused the mare. Her ears pricked up, conveying her emotion to the female.

"I'm happy too." The female smiled. "Now, what is your name, for I doubt it is Ball Breaker?"

The mare gave a shrill whinny and pawed the ground.

"They did not give you a proper name? How rude. We must address that immediately. How about something from my homeland? Would you accept Blizzard? For your run is truly blinding."

Jacob stood, slack-jawed as the formerly cantankerous mount dipped her head in what he swore was agreement.

"Will you be so kind as to return to your stall? I will follow in a moment to rub you down."

Head held high, the newly named horse trotted back to her stall.

Jacob watched the mysterious horse whisperer dismount the railing like an old cowhand.

"Should I ask how you managed that?"

"Probably not, you wouldn't believe me anyway."

Jacob nodded and left the two of them to get better acquainted. For some inexplicable reason, he felt like a third wheel.

He trudged back to the patio vowing that, before she disappeared, he would get her to teach him that trick.

CHAPTER

NINETEEN

By the end of the month, Freya was firmly entrenched in Jacob's life. She often disappeared for hours riding Blizzard through the fields and, lately, among the buffalo.

While they paid little attention to her intrusion, Jacob knew it would not take much to change that situation.

Instead of waiting for the inevitable, he decided to take matters into his own hands.

He had already learned the hard way that saying 'no' was a waste of breath. His chef's kitchen bore the scars of the mini blaze she had triggered when cooking him breakfast.

How she managed to set fire to a pot of boiling water escaped him.

Aware that putting her to work in his diner in town would likely end up with her burning the place down, he collected on an age-old debt with the owner of the bookstore down the street from the diner.

From merchants to ranchers, almost everyone in town was in debt to Jacob. If there was a roof to patch, a calf to be delivered, or a fence to be mended, Jacob was the man to see.

If payment was ever mentioned, and it rarely was, he declined with a smile, saying it was ok to settle later. Except *later* never came around.

Until today...

Jacob had built the bookshelves in Becca's shop and deemed it time to *inspect* them.

Needless to say, Becca was surprised to find him propped against the door jamb when she opened for business.

"Why, Jacob Deerstin, what brings you to my humble shop so early in the morning? Surely can't be the coffee. Can't compare with yours."

"Thought I'd just check to see whether those shelves I built ya are still standing."

The peculiar remark prompted a baffled shrug as she led him through the seating area of the bookstore, which consisted of a hodgepodge of mismatched chairs and tables, as well as a stray accent chair or two.

Including his great-grandmother's wooden rocker.

Jacob smiled inwardly whenever he passed it. He pictured her withered body perched on its worn black leather cushion, while she regaled her grandson with the history of his people.

These days, Becca sat in it to read stories to the local children on Saturday mornings.

He knew it pleased the old woman to see it put to good use.

The rich aroma of freshly brewed coffee permeated the bookstore as they walked through to where the books were displayed — *displayed* being a loose term for Becca's organizational skills.

A former librarian, she detested the Dewey Decimal System. In her opinion, books should be arranged by interests.

Meaning, with the exception of the rare first editions she held under lock and key in the case, Jacob had built behind the counter, the remainder of her eclectic collection of old and new books were spread about on the tables and shelves in the sales area.

While, to anyone else, it resembled the handiwork of a madwoman, to Becca, it made perfect sense. In less time than it took to locate a particular book using her computer system, she could retrieve it, ring it up, and have it bagged and waiting.

Everyone has a special talent.

As they reached the stacks — built, stained, and sealed by Jacob — he ran expert fingers along the wood, checking for nicks and splinters.

Observing him for a couple of minutes, Becca said, "Look, Jacob, I'm not sure what you're up to, but the Women's Book Club is about to descend *en masse*, and I don't have time for guessing games."

Jacob took a step back and whistled, "Yep, they will no doubt stand for a hundred years. Probably outlast this old build—"

Becoming a little agitated with her friend, Becca demanded, "Jacob, out with it, now."

"I need a favor, hon."

"You finally came to collect, eh? Business dropped off that much at the diner? If you need payment for the shelves, you're going to have to give me some leeway. We haven't hit the tourist season yet, so money is a little tight. Say a month—"

"Oh, I'm not asking for anything that drastic," Jacob

interrupted at the worried look on Becca's face. "I'm hoping you have a part time job available."

"For you? I didn't think you were interested in books."

"I'm not. I've got too many stories swirling around up here, thanks to Great-Grandma Chenoa..." he joked, tapping the side of his head, "...the job is for a friend."

"Ahhh, I heard one of the ladies in the club talking about a woman hiding out at your place."

"Trust me, Becca, *hiding* is the wrong word," Jacob lamented. "Need to put her somewhere before she wrecks my ranch."

"So, you want to drop her in my shop, eh?" Becca's Minnesotan-Norwegian coloring her tone. "And here I thought you liked me."

"Please, Becca," Jacob begged. "She's highly intelligent, and I'm positive the two of you will hit it off."

Becca's expression informed Jacob, she was not convinced.

"And... I'll fix anything she breaks."

The front doorbell rang to announce the arrival of the Book Club who would be anticipating coffee as steamy as the book Becca was about to suggest.

"Fine, bring her by tomorrow and we'll see. Now, get on with you, before I give you the boot."

Jacob laughed and kissed Becca on the forehead. "You're a saint, hon."

"No, I'm an eejit for dealin' with the devil."

The next morning, as promised, Jacob and Freya were waiting for Becca at the entrance to the bookstore.

To sweeten the disposition of Freya's prospective new

employer, the pair came armed with fresh pastries from the local bakery and a large thermos of Jacob's specially blended coffee.

It was a family recipe handed down to him by his mother, under the threat of haunting him should he ever divulge her secret.

Becca shook her head at the obvious bribe as they followed her in.

"Have a seat, you two, I'll go fetch some cups."

Freya watched the woman disappear into the back.

Turning to Jacob, she sighed. "She hates me already."

"For Pete's sake, Freda, she hasn't even met you yet. You have to give her time to work up to hating you."

Freya smacked his arm as he laughed.

"*If* I hire you," Becca said casually as she returned, "there will be no hanky-panky in the stacks. I run a respectable business here, not some kind of teen makeout spot for the two of you."

Becca's tease triggered the image of a certain Irish bartender and the times they spent canoodling in not so secluded places.

The memory elicited a rare blush, something which hadn't occurred since her time with Sean.

With effort, Freya pushed the memory of the strapping Irishman into her checkered past.

"I can assure you, Mrs—"

"That's Ms."

Is this woman deliberately trying to embarrass me? Freya pondered.

"Forgive me, Ms. Swenson—"

"Most people call me Becca."

What in Niflheim is up with her?

With a huff, Freya corrected herself, "*Becca*... I guarantee that won't be an issue."

Both women glanced at Jacob, who stopped mid-drink, unsure what he had just missed.

Setting his cup down, he asked nervously, "What?"

Waving her friend off, Becca focused on Freya, her tone, less serious.

"Isn't he cute with that *deer-in-the-headlights* look?" Becca laughed, nodding her head at Jacob.

Leaning her elbows on the table, she twinkled. "Though watching your face flare into such a fiery shade is just as fun.

"Back to the matter at hand. Have you ever worked in a bookstore before? It's not really a glamorous life... unless stocking shelves and filling coffee cups floats your boat."

"Can't say I've ever done more than read... although I do fancy myself as a bit of an historian," Freya informed the shopkeeper, a hint of pride in her reply. "In fact, recently, I volunteered at a museum."

"Really, which one?" Becca quizzed.

Even if the woman did not work out as an assistant, Becca was excited to find someone else who might share the same interests.

Unwilling to expand on her time in the Emerald Isle, Freya hedged, "I doubt you've ever been there or have even heard of it, for that matter. It's in Dublin. It is a quaint little place though."

Understatement of the year.

"Well, whatever," Becca said, setting that aside for another day. "If Jacob is willing to vouch for your character..."

Freya's preemptive kick to Jacob's shin curbed the snide

comment she knew hovered on the tip of his tongue about her being a character, with painful effect.

"...you can start with a couple of days a week, and we'll see how it goes. Fair enough?"

Freya smiled and extended her hand to Becca, "I'll become indispensable, trust me."

"I'll be happy if you don't get crushed under an avalanche of books."

Rubbing his shin, Jacob excused himself. "I've got to open the diner, so I'll leave the two of you to whatever bookstore people do.

"Oh, and Freda, come over to the diner for dinner after work. I'll make you something special to celebrate your new job... *and* we can talk about your rent."

"And here am I thinking cleaning up after you was payment enough."

With a wolfish grin, Jacob vanished through the door.

As the small bell chimed his exit, Freya mused, *I'm not sure which governs me more... my head, heart, or stomach? Who am I kidding? It explains why I am always attracted to those damn restaurateurs.*

With the man gone, Becca decided to pin down her new employee's relationship with Jacob. "Don't forget what I told you two about the stacks."

"For the last time, Becca, we've only held hands once, and that was to keep me from falling on my derriere getting out of his truck, and I'm beginning to think that's as far as it will ever go."

Freya's confession saddened Becca.

"Give him time, girl. He's a bit slow on the uptake. Now, how about we see whether I made the right choice in letting him blackmail me into hiring you."

CHAPTER

TWENTY

To Becca's surprise and relief, business at the bookstore flourished. The start of the tourist season brought an unexpected influx of customers, seeking reading material to keep themselves occupied during the endless miles from western Montana, across the Dakotas and into Minnesota.

Gaining a new friend, an added bonus.

The two swapped travel stories, although Becca was envious that Freda's international jaunt had included half of Europe, whereas hers ended just over the Canadian border at the International Peace Gardens.

Freda's vivid descriptions of the places she had visited made Becca feel as though she had experienced them with her.

Despite this, the older woman sensed there were details, her new friend withheld deliberately.

Case in point was when Becca had pressed Freda about her time volunteering at the 'quaint' Dublin Museum.

The history books they were stacking, had prompted Becca's, "Ya know, I've actually been to the Dublin museum in Ohio. It was okay but nothing to write home about."

"Really? I have not seen it, so cannot disavow your opinion. The National Museum of Ireland - Archaeology in *that* Dublin, on the other hand, is quite another matter. The corridors I trod as a tour guide..."

Too late, Freda realized she had been a little too liberal with her information.

Smoothly, she switched to an amusing tale about a drinking contest with the Bürgermeister of Munich during an Oktoberfest many years ago.

Not easily diverted, Becca pressed, "How did you manage to visit so many countries, Freda?"

Freda's reply was a cryptic, "It's all about who you know."

Becca was nothing if not sensitive and, recognizing Freda was not going to be drawn, made a mental note not to broach the topic again. Instead, the two women spent their time cultivating their friendship, as well as their business.

Over the past couple of years, as a way to encourage parents to bring their kids to the bookshop on Saturdays, Becca had featured story time.

Now, with Freda alongside, this had become something of a theater of the mind. The pair co-read the books, and impersonated the voices of the various characters.

The attendance quadrupled.

In appreciation for Freda's help, Becca promoted her to full-time assistant manager.

To say Jacob was ecstatic to learn his roommate was now being watched the entire day, and not left to her own devices, gained Becca the promise of a hand hewn, oak, French Provincial writing desk.

Becca was not one to look a gift horse in the mouth.

The one problem which arose from Freya's employment was that she ended up loitering in the diner until it closed.

To stave off boredom, she often bussed tables. She *had* tried to worm her way onto the prep line, but Jacob was quick to escort her out of the kitchen and back to waitressing.

The regulars enjoyed the banter between the two, with some questioning whether Jacob had bought a mail order bride just to keep himself occupied.

He let them go on thinking that way, because it seemed to encourage more couples to come to the diner on 'date night' to enjoy the free comedic entertainment.

As smoothly as Jacob could hope, this continued, until the night Freya had to wait longer than usual for Jacob to finish his shift.

The diner was bustling when Freya entered but, after a busy day at the bookshop, she was too tired to help out. *I need a break. Keeping those rambunctious kids together today was worse than herding my damn cats.*

Grabbing a pot of Jacob's elixir... his richly brewed coffee... and a cup, Freya — so as not to waste any of the staff's time trying to serve her — found an empty table in a corner, within view of the counter, but away from the popular tables.

Her efforts failed miserably.

A surly looking trucker happened by Freya's table on the way back from the men's room.

Spotting the exotic bombshell sitting unattended, he decided to make himself at home next to her in the booth.

Sliding an arm around her shoulders, he dared make a play for her.

"Hey, doll, why don't you blow this popsicle stand and explore the country with me. I could use some eye-candy like you in my cab. You'd be hard pushed to catch your breath with the excitement, I could show you."

Before Freya could extract herself and reduce the gorilla to a pile of ash, Jacob was out from behind the counter, using a thumb grasp he had learned in the military to break the man's hold, nearly destroying the trucker's digit in the process.

Free of the man's unwelcome advance, Freya tried to calm the situation, "Jacob, it's okay. No harm, no foul."

Jacob would have none of it. With the man under his control, Jacob lifted the unwanted guest to his feet.

"I think it's time you hit the road," he informed the driver, an ominous undertone telling anyone listening that he was serious.

"I'm not done eating, and I haven't finished my conversation with Ms. Cutie-pie here, *gramps*."

It was true, Jacob had about twenty years on the man, but that was no reason to back down.

"Last time, bub, leave quietly or the two of us are going to step outside to settle your bill once for all."

Freya stood in awe as the confrontation continued. She had grown used to men fighting for the right to bed her.

Just boys hyped up on testosterone, was her considered opinion of Midgardian males.

Watching Jacob, elicited a completely different sentiment.

For the first time, a man was willing to defend her honor. While Sean was cut from the same cloth, to witness it in action, made her heart flutter.

"Fine, fine. I'm going," the trucker capitulated through gritted teeth. "Just give me back my damn thumb. Cheap move."

Keeping his eye on the guy, Jacob relaxed his fingers, and waited for the trucker to leave.

Not the smartest tool in the shed, the man decided to test his luck, and risked a sly jab at Jacob.

The next thing the trucker saw was the ceiling, his jaw throbbing from Jacob's flying fist, and Jacob standing over him, grinning triumphantly. "Not too shabby for an old man.

"Get him out of here." This to the two burly cooks who hoisted the stunned man upright and frog-marched him to his truck.

This time, the trucker thought it wise to follow his, sadly negligible, common sense.

Jacob barked, "Freda, my office. **Now**."

In that instant, all of Jacob's chivalry vanished before Freya's eyes.

"Why? I was the victim here," she grumbled.

"Don't argue, just move."

Muttering dire threats under her breath, she did as he bade.

*All men **are** the same. Brutes, the lot of 'em.*

Once the door closed behind them, Jacob's attitude softened.

"Look, hon, you're too goddamned beautiful for me to fight off every swinging dick who walks through the door."

Did he just call me hon... and say I was beautiful? was all Freya registered.

"Next weekend, you and I are going to the reservation's used car auction. I'd rather have you waiting for me at home when you get off work, than chase every male customer out of the diner."

Beautiful? That word replayed in her brain like a long-distance echo.

Freya watched Jacob's lips move but heard nothing else. When he stopped, she nodded her head in agreement.

As it had with Sean... this seemed to placate him, and she knew they would revisit whatever it was he was going on about soon enough.

The morning weather girl promised a bright, sunny Saturday and, for once, did not fail to deliver.

By nine o'clock, the thermometer read 87°, which gave Freya a legitimate excuse to wear oversized sunglasses and her infamous Greek floppy hat to the auction.

Jacob, on the other hand, could not help but observe, "Ya know, you'd have been less conspicuous wearing a bikini than that get up."

"Can't be too careful. We don't know whether the reservation police are still looking for me. Besides, I burn easily, and I've spent eons trying to look this good."

An odd turn of phrase, but Jacob was becoming accustomed to Freya's... eccentricities.

The pair strolled through the line-up of cars before the auction started. Periodically, Jacob stopped to check under the hood of some vehicle, which Freya immediately dismissed after a single glance through the driver's window.

"Ya know, Freda, none of these are new cars. Best you can hope for is finding one without a nest of rats living in the front seat."

"You make a lousy used car salesman, Mr. Deerstin."

Jacob grinned, shrugged, and moved to the next one.

Eventually, as the heat crept from searing to intolerable, the couple reached the last row of offerings. These were cars the auction had listed as requiring TLC.

Which, of course, is exactly where Freya found her pride and joy. A blue and black 1970 Mercury Cougar.

The car had definitely seen better days. It was dirty but, to Freya's delight, the interior was intact, just needing detailing... *thoroughly*.

It was Jacob's responsibility to check out the mechanics. Popping the hood, he was surprised to find it came with the legendary Boss 302 Eliminator engine package, which Freya fired up on her second turn of the key.

"See... she wants me to take her home," Freya exhorted.

Trying to persuade Jacob of the Cougar's worth, Freya pressed the accelerator, causing the old girl to sputter, and spit out a dark cloud from the tailpipe.

Jacob's experienced ear recognized the tappets singing their sad, out-of-tune story denoting an abused powertrain.

"Hon, I gotta tell you, she's had a rough trot. No doubt some kid's been street racing the poor girl."

"Pish," Freya dismissed his concerns. "Nothing a little elbow grease, and your special talent, can't fix."

"Get that sweet butt of yours out of the car and let me check something," he ordered.

Begrudgingly, not wanting to relinquish her position behind the wheel, she did as he asked.

He checked the clutch and shifter assembly. As he expected, the clutch was torched, and the gear shift was as useless as the pine tree air freshener hanging from the mirror.

"You know we passed a really nice Vista Cruiser up front, in way better shape than this heap."

"Are you kidding me?" Freya scoffed. "Do I look like a mom needing a grocery getter to you?"

"You do know that car has a bigger engine than this one and can go faster."

"But. It. Is. Still. A. Station. Wagon," Freya retorted, succinctly.

"But it will require less—"

"I'm buying this one and that's all there is to it," she finished the conversation with her arms folded.

"Fine, but you're responsible for getting this piece of shit back to the ranch, and do you even know how to drive a stick? To be fair, it *does* take exceptional talent to park sideways in a ditch."

"That was an extenuating circumstance, and I have you to teach me, don't I?" Her face bloomed into a smile only the goddess of seduction could achieve. One, no man could resist.

Freya and Jacob tried to look disinterested in the vehicle as a group of bidders traipsed after the auctioneer to where the Mercury sat.

The auctioneer wasted little time in praising her beyond the fact it had a special package under the hood, and there had only been a few thousand of these cars to roll off the assembly line.

"How about we start the bidding at two grand." An offer no one bit on.

'Five hundred," a voice behind Freya called out.

"I have five, do I have six?" The auctioneer lit up.

Jacob glanced at the man, recognizing him as a dealer with a reputation for buying classics, cleaning them up, and selling them overseas as antiques. Shonky as all get out.

Jacob nodded for six.

"Seven-fifty," the guy countered.

"Five thousand!"

The entire auction fell silent as all eyes swivelled to the diminutive blonde waving a handful of cash.

"What the hell are you doing?" Jacob hissed. "That's not how auctions work."

"It does when I want something," she whispered from the corner of her mouth.

Jacob looked at the dealer, who ignored him.

"Congratulations, little lady, you just bought yourself a true hotrod," the auctioneer informed Freya, not bothering to hide his glee at getting the hunk of junk off his property.

"Make sure to see the ladies in the office for the title work and to make arrangements to have your new car delivered to wherever you want it."

The crowd around them remained speechless in stunned disbelief at what they had just witnessed.

Some thought it a poor display of auction etiquette, while others attributed it to heat stroke.

As for Jacob, his lingering question for the woman he was following to the tin-roofed shack was, "Are you ever going to tell me where this endless supply of cash you have comes from?"

Without slowing down or glancing back, Freya replied airily, "Probably not."

Adding softly, "I don't actually know myself."

TWENTY-ONE

The following Saturday saw the couple in Jacob's barn examining the partially disassembled remains of the vehicle, Freya had affectionately dubbed Oskar — to the disdain of Jacob.

"Why did you give the poor thing a man's name? Hasn't this car already suffered enough humiliation?"

"What in the world are you going on about? I think Oskar is a very regal name. In Norse, it means faster than a divine spear."

"Which is why no one... with the exception of history nerds like you... speak Norse anymore. Besides, ships and cars are supposed to be named after women."

"That's terrible. Why would anybody want to drive a woman so hard for enjoyment..." she stopped and gave Jacob a knowing look, aware it was a question wasted on a man.

"Moving on, Mr. Deerstin, how about you shimmy under my car and check out the transmission linkage."

Freya had no idea what she was talking about but, she had spent the last week reading up on auto repair at the bookstore, and wanted to impress the grizzled mechanic with her technical smarts.

"Sure, and while I'm doing that, would you mind digging through my toolbox for my half-inch left-handed torque wrench?"

"But I thought you were right-handed?"

"I am, but I have to take the bolts off the left side of the block."

"Oh... that makes sense."

Jacob grinned wickedly and watched as she sauntered to the tool cabinet.

Occasionally, while digging through the box, Freya dangled a random tool over her shoulder. "This is it, right?"

To which, Jacob identified it correctly, and suggested she try the next drawer down.

It was not until Freya knelt to scrounge through the bottom drawer, did Jacob say, "Oh, that's right, it's under the car already."

Truth be told, he was enjoying the sight of Freda's skintight cutoff denim shorts cup her supple butt, the further down she went.

In Freda's current position, Jacob was convinced of the ancient adage, a woman's perfect ass resembles an inverted heart.

At least on Freda it did.

The sudden silence from Jacob prompted Freya to glance over her shoulder to catch a stupid grin on Jacob's face.

Realization dawned, eliciting an exasperated eye roll and a terse, "You're so juvenile."

Getting to her feet, she joined him, leaning over the fender to watch Jacob slide under the Mercury where he began to examine the beaten-up transmission.

It did not take him long to accept he was in over his head. He considered suggesting they swap out the old powertrain for a new 350 engine and transmission, but was sure her eye for authenticity would not allow for anything less than the parts the workers in Dearborn, Michigan had shoehorned into the beast.

Looking up through the bits and pieces of the engine, he gave her the bad news.

"He's shot, hon."

Freya pouted, "Nooooo. Is nothing salvageable?"

"Short of sinking it into the nearest pond, there's only one person, I can think of who might be able to save it."

"Great, get them over here."

Jacob sighed, "You don't understand, the last person I want to be in debt to is my own brother."

"Suck it up, buttercup." Freya giggled.

Jacob heard the car door open, as Freya climbed inside.

She called to him, "Come up here and join me, and I'll show you how appreciative I am for all you've done."

Scurrying out from below, Jacob opened the door, to get hit in the face with Freya's T-shirt.

Startled, he pulled the top from his head and stared at it in confusion, then his gaze lifted.

In front of him... a topless goddess.

Shamelessly, she offered her hand to him.

Without a second's thought, he took it and was dragged into the cramped back seat with her.

The couple attempted to consummate their mutual attraction, quickly coming to the conclusion, they were too old to act like teenagers. Buck-naked, they spilled out of the Mercury, racing to Jacob's bedroom and his California-king bed.

Panting from their mad dash, Freya giggled wildly,

making Jacob swear, "*Do not* let Becca know what just happened. I seriously do not think I could stand the humiliation of explaining it to her."

"Deal... now seduce me."

He did...

...and again on the famous, handmade kitchen table... the couch... in front of the fireplace... ending up in Freya's bed.

Which was where Jacob's brother, Randy, found them when he walked in unannounced.

Leaning against the bedroom door, his shrill whistle woke them from an exhausted slumber. Jacob jumped from the bed, while Freya hid under the covers.

"Christ, Randy, do you know what a doorbell is?"

"Got tired of ringing it... and, from your breathless call, I thought you might be having a heart attack."

Jacob began his cross-examination, "*When* did I call you exactly?"

As the words left his lips, Jacob remembered making a hurried call, between rounds, asking Randy to come over and bring his truck.

Trying to turn it back on his brother, he huffed, "And I'd be dead by now if I *was* having one."

"From your beet red face, I'm afraid it may still be a possibility. I'm guessing the lump under the covers is responsible for your present condition."

Peering around his naked brother, Randy chuckled and said to the hidden occupant, "While my etiquette-challenged, older brother sees fit to get dressed, allow me to introduce myself. Randall Lee Deerstin at your service."

A hand and slender arm snaked out from under to covers to wave a greeting.

"Freda Odinson. Nice to meet you."

"I'm here to collect something... though Jacob here was a little cryptic. So, if you will allow me, I'm going to drag him out to see what I'm getting myself into."

Feeling Jacob yank on his arm, Randy left Freya with an invitation, "Come out and join us when you find your clothes."

From the hallway, Freya heard Jacob instruct, "Jeans... already gonna owe this idiot enough for fixing the Cougar. There's no reason to give him a free peep show to boot."

The brothers were in the barn prepping the car for its trip on Randy's flatbed tow truck.

Both turned in unison as Freya called to them, "Either of you want a Guinness?"

Jacob was about to reiterate to Randy, his low opinion of the thick brew when the pair of them lost the ability to function.

Before them stood the goddess of seduction in a floral sundress.

The bodice dipped ever so slightly, exposing the merest hint of her full breasts, the spaghetti strings striving to maintain her modesty as they clung to her shoulders. The early evening breeze teased about the hem of her skirt.

In her hands, she held out two chilled Blue Ribbons.

She gave a cheeky giggle. "Gotcha!

"And, Randy, if you would be so kind as to put your tongue to better use, and tell me how you're gonna resurrect my car."

CHAPTER

TWENTY-TWO

In the room she had commandeered when Jacob first brought her to Wise River, Freya stood back to admire herself in the full-length, slightly de-silvered mirror, in its aged frame. The mirror, Jacob informed her, had once belonged to his grandmother — like so many of his treasured items.

She turned this way and that, making sure the dress was sitting just right.

Never in her wildest dreams did she imagine she would see this day... conveniently forgetting a certain handfasting ceremony performed when she was a giddy, dewy-eyed, young goddess with no real clue as to the long-term ramifications of the ritual.

A smile curved her lips as her mind wandered back over the previous months.

Freya had believed she was on the cusp of falling in love with Sean. Her affection for the Irishman had far exceeded the sentiment she felt for Loki... the only other man who, prior to Sean, had touched her heart.

How little she knew.

The night Jacob rescued her from the ditch — for, in retrospect, she recognized she had actually fallen in love with him at first sight — was the night everything changed.

The gruff, rather taciturn rancher had sparked an emotion completely foreign to Freya. Unselfishness.

All she wanted was his happiness and, if that meant she had to compromise, so be it.

That's not to say it was all sunshine and rainbows. Freya owned a spirited temperament, and they sparred frequently, their arguments becoming legendary, but they blew over quickly — usually because Jacob kissed her into silence.

For the first time since she had witnessed Sela and Loki's nauseating rapture, Freya understood the sheer depth of their connection.

Of course, the bond Jacob and I have is stronger, she mused smugly.

She recalled the day Jacob proposed.

She was messing about, posing like the women she had seen on the posters in Randy's workshop.

Stretching languidly on the newly waxed hood of her repaired, serviced, cleaned, and tuned up Cougar, whose highly polished blue and black paint glittered in the sunlight.

"Freya," Jacob warned, "you'll look like crispy bacon if you don't get down."

Freya rolled onto her stomach, one leg straight out, one leg angled upward at the knee, foot twirling. She crooked her finger invitingly.

"Come here and get me, lover," she crooned.

Smothering a laugh, Jacob assumed a cowboy swagger and strutted to the car.

"Now, little lady," he said out of the corner of his mouth. "How's about I take you somewhere to cool off?"

He swung her off the hood and, as he stood her on her feet, she shimmied down his body with calculated deliberation.

His breathing hitched. "Temptress," he rasped.

Lifting onto her tiptoes, she smiled and brushed her lips to his. "You were saying…"

Jacob took her hands and, suddenly, it was as though the world had stilled. With all the chivalry he had demonstrated time and time again, Jacob dropped onto one knee.

Freya's heart hammered in her chest.

"Freda Odinson, you are the most intransigent, disruptive, exasperating, and wilful woman I have ever known."

Freya frowned… *wait what*…? She opened her mouth to refute his assertion.

"Hush," he said, before she could get a word in.

"As I was saying… wilful woman,I have ever known. You barreled into my life on the wings of a storm, like a valkyrie of old, and turned it upside down. An insurgence, I was not ready for has become the battlefield I would die on—"

Arms folded, Freya ignored his reference to Odin's winged witches, raised a brow, and tapped her foot. "Insurgency? Battlefield?"

"Hush," he repeated. "Freda, I love you. I love you beyond reason and logic, and can think of no higher honor than spending the rest of my life wrangling with you to prove just how much.

"Will you marry me?"

Freya's jaw dropped, as the wisp of something wholly

indefinable blossomed in her core and coiled out along her veins.

He loved her.

She knew his affection ran deep, but to hear him enunciate it so unequivocally, humbled and thrilled her.

She tilted her head, to study him, reading a guardedness in his eyes.

Despite all the sensible and very pertinent arguments to the contrary, bouncing around her head, there was never any question.

"***Yes***!" she squealed and leaped into his arms, her legs hooking around his waist.

Their betrothal was sealed with fiery passion.

Since Jacob's proposal, Freya had become aware of a curious contentment, as though everything in her long existence had been some convoluted form of preparation.

That all the chaos, anguish, and torment, the numerous challenges she had faced and overcome were part of a deliberate plan created — clearly, by someone with a warped sense of humor... she was going with Fate — in order for her to appreciate the unconditional, unadorned, and indissoluble love, she shared with Jacob.

She was about to bind herself to someone... a mortal from Midgard, no less... for all eternity and she could not wait.

The mirror flickered, distorting her image. Startled, Freya blinked, and squinted at the glass which seemed to be liquifying.

For a split second, she contemplated whether this was an earthquake.

Jacob had told her that small ones were not uncommon, although most people didn't even register they were happening, so that explanation was improbable.

Something else then...

...slowly, the ripples smoothed, but another face stared back at her. A hostile face whose frosty blue eye skewered her as painfully as though it was a dagger.

Odin.

This did not bode well.

With supreme effort, Freya masked her trepidation, and watched Odin's expression morph into one of incredulity.

"A white dress, virginal attire." His laughter held no humor. "*Virginal...* which idiot..." he stopped and Freya could almost see the cogs of his mind grinding.

She kept her features smooth to the point of boredom.

"You did not heed my warning."

"And, *I* seem to recall reminding you that you cannot interfere in this realm." She strove for nonchalance.

"Your affection for these ignorant humans has addled your already irresponsible and irrational brain."

His eyes looked beyond her to scan the room.

"You think you can scurry away like a tawdry thief and hide him from me?"

"I *never* scurry," Freya's chin went up.

"Where is the pup? Do not think you can protect him."

"He is not here."

That, at least, was the truth.

At this moment, Randy was driving Jacob into town, then coming back for her.

"Just because he claims Viking heritage is not enough to avert the consequences. Do not push me, Freya. If you flout the rules and marry him — *marry him... pah* — 'I do,' will be the last words he utters."

Shocked, Freya realized Odin assumed she was marrying Sean. It was as though there was a time lag in Valhalla.

Was that possible?

Freya did not know, but was in no hurry to apprise him of her change in circumstance.

What Odin did not know, saved Jacob.

Her brain worked furiously.

Can I outwit him?

She had to try.

Employing every ounce of wit and guile, Freya tried to distract Odin from his purpose, to no avail. The longer it went on, the colder she felt.

This was an encounter, she could not win.

Her heart cracked.

Just when a lifetime of bliss was within her grasp, the damn Asgardian was going to snatch it away.

Hatred warred with devastation.

She could not, in all conscience... another first for her... hurt Jacob. Yet, whatever she did now, would result in exactly that.

"How do you suppose, he will feel seeing you remain in your prime, while he withers and dies, or will you allow yourself to 'age' with him?" Odin sniped. "You cannot make him immortal."

Freya's shoulders sagged.

The agony of knowing she would lose Jacob... one way or another... crushed her soul, but she had an ace up her sleeve.

Odin did not know about Jacob. He still assumed she was marrying Sean.

She *could* save him, even if that meant forfeiting her own happiness. At least he had the chance to live a full life, maybe find another love.

Her heart fractured.

Just your typical rock and hard place, she snarked inwardly.

There was no time. No time to tell him why, no time to say goodbye, no time to tell him she loved him more than her own life.

A twinge of guilt hit her, with the realization she was delegating the dubious task of breaking Jacob's heart to his own brother.

Freya could already imagine the phone call between Randy and Jacob, after the younger brother returned to find the house missing the excited bride.

Though she held out hope that Randy would find a more tactful way of doing so than, "Bro, she's gone."

Forcing all that aside, she looked Odin in the eye.

"Fine, old man. You win. Do not..." as a sardonic smile began to curve his cruel mouth, "...take this as capitulation. It is merely the lesser of two evils."

"Do not make me regret my munificence."

The image started to fade, and the last thing Freya saw was his cold, hard, implacable eye.

Her heart shattered.

TWENTY-THREE

reya questioned whether her life was being sucked into a vortex. In fact, a vortex would be preferable to the debacle in which she was now involved.

Cryptic instructions imparted telepathically by an unborn child was preposterous enough. To follow said instructions while trying to avoid detection by another god, his witch of a wife... who also happened to be the child's mother, Odin, his Valkyries, and any number of supernatural creatures was farcical.

In fact, had she been watching this on television, Freya would be rolling her eyes and laughing incredulously.

Adding insult to injury, this summons — which necessitated a side trip to Valhalla on the pretext of demanding a divorce but was, in reality, a ruse to obtain information, and where an inadvertent slip of the tongue had nearly wrecked the whole scheme — had granted her no time to grieve her abrupt departure from Wise River and the love of her life.

Tears threatened, but she blinked rapidly. *Not the time to show any weakness*, she admonished herself. *This mission is crucial. If I fail, we are doomed... all of us in every realm are doomed.*

Despite her lingering antagonism towards Sela, Freya would die to prevent any harm being inflicted on the woman's child whose protection was paramount.

Several times, en route, she tried to warn Sela but, although she knew the latter had registered the caution, it spurred her on rather than sent her home.

In all honesty, given the rapid dissembling of Odin's mind, Freya didn't know where Sela was safer.

It was only when she saw the sign for Montreal that Freya recognized where they were headed.

"Risky move, Loki, risky move. You are cutting it fine."

Getting there before Sela gave birth would be touch and go and, although probably the only place out of Odin's reach, Freya knew Sela's fate if she stayed in Loki's home dimension.

Using her powers, Freya could catch and warn the couple ahead of her with ease, but that would reveal her position to those sly Valkyries who had the ear of Odin.

This required stealth not sorcery.

It seemed Nature was determined to stall her, throwing everything at her, but she persevered, and crept onto the ferry, bound for Newfoundland, at North Sydney unnoticed by either Sela or Loki... although it was a close thing.

When the ferry docked, she loitered at Port aux Basques until the guttural roar of Sela's coupe faded to a muffled hum.

She patted the steering wheel of her beloved Oskar. "She wouldn't know a classic car if it ran over her," she assured the Cougar.

Weary from the long journey, and cognizant of the

destination, she did not hurry, taking time to eat, and refuel the car.

Shortly thereafter, she pointed Oskar at L'Anse aux Meadows.

The next few days tested Freya in ways she could never have imagined.

On top of abandoning Jacob with no explanation, she had driven halfway across Canada, planted her precious car in a snowdrift, and saved the life of her erstwhile best friend, only to watch the man she once believed to be her soul mate, die a gruesome death at the hands of the deranged Asgardian.

Now, she was in a desperate battle to keep Anna — a baby who possessed more power than the entire Norse pantheon put together — hidden until she could find a safe haven.

Masking the infant's power was no small feat, and Freya was tiring, heart break at the compounding losses undermining her usual indomitable strength.

Worse, Sela blamed her for Loki's death and the target on her newborn's head. While understandable, the younger woman's fury left Freya fearing for her own life.

Yet, the fate of the trio was inextricably linked.

As their seemingly random journey took them south, the tension between Freya and Sela evaporated, supplanted by a mutual desire to guard Anna and, slowly, a friendship was rekindled.

There was only one person in this godforsaken land, Freya trusted. The same person she had left at the altar, whose hopes and dreams she had destroyed, mere weeks ago.

She had no alternative.

It was the hardest thing Freya had ever done, but she swallowed her pride to plead for sanctuary.

The chivalry, Freya relied on, came to the fore and Jacob, while harboring a smoldering fury, was not going to ignore the plight of a new mother and her baby.

What began as a grudging agreement to provide a room for a couple of nights, quickly morphed into a permanent arrangement.

Jacob's antipathy abated until, one day, he realized he would always love Freya, that holding a grudge and being righteously angry was a waste of time. Time which could be spent in much better ways... not that he was in any hurry to apprise Freya of his epiphany... enjoying her determination to atone.

Freya, keenly aware of Jacob's softening, remained apparently oblivious, happy and relieved they were reaching common ground. Secretly, she hoped they might be afforded a second chance.

Weeks became months and stretched into years.

. . .

Freya and Sela believed they were successful in concealing their whereabouts, until a hunting trip caused an unforeseen mistake, which although had catastrophic results, proved a catalyst for Freya and Jacob.

Their smoldering ardor could be denied no longer and, in an unassuming motel on the outskirts of Baker, Montana, Freya made a goddess-changing decision... at the same time as Sela burst through the connecting door... without knocking.

"Freya, Anna says we need to leave right n—"

"Dammit, Sela." Freya dragged the comforter around her. "Perfect timing as usual. What do you want?"

Ignoring Sela's obvious embarrassment, Freya listened to the younger woman's harried explanation about yet another horror unfolding.

She blew a long sigh as Sela tried to tug her out of bed. "Come on, get dressed, we cannot tarry."

"I'm not going, Sela. I'm done." Freya glanced at Jacob who smiled his slow tender smile, making her heart melt. "I belong here," her words were soft and rang with conviction."

Sela gaped, uncomprehendingly. "Well, that's all fine and dandy, but what will this," she gestured between the two, "matter if Loki implements what Anna saw?" Sela's question was bitter, her disappointment plain.

"Then I'll die with the man I love," Freya replied. "All stories come to an end, eventually... don't they? Maybe this is just my Happily Ever After."

"Freya, how can you stand by without lifting a finger? It's not okay to let everyone die because you prefer to indulge in a grand romance," Sela hissed.

In less than a heartbeat Freya was beside Sela, clasping her hands. Concentrating, she locked eyes with her friend and relinquished her power, sensing it diminish then surge through Sela's body.

The pair was engulfed in the purest of Nature's energy. It lifted them from the floor, suspending them in time and space.

Freya channeled everything she possessed into Sela.

As, almost, the last vestiges of her magic flowed out, Freya experienced a wave of relief so intense, she was surprised no one else saw it, and felt Sela kiss her on the cheek as they landed gently on the floor.

Drawing her friend into a fierce hug, Freya whispered, "Go save us."

EPILOGUE

Three Months Later

Sela leaned her hip against the massive table in Jacob's kitchen, and scratched her head. Planning the wedding breakfast for a goddess had sounded great in theory, in practice it was becoming a bit of a headache.

"I must have been out of my mind," she muttered to the empty room.

While Freya and Jacob preferred a small wedding, they were determined to include all those who had rallied around to help rebuild the ranch and the diner.

Finger food would not suffice.

What on earth can I do that's different?

Jacob was an amazing chef. Anything, she produced would be pathetic... and quite possibly poisonous by comparison. An irreverent giggle surfaced as she pictured

Jacob's wrath when he discovered she had tried to kill off his fiancée... however accidentally.

She could hear him bellowing now, "If you think dying on me will excuse you from marrying me, think again, Freya Odinson. I will hunt you into the afterlife."

Setting that amusing image aside, Sela tried to concentrate. In truth, since Freya had transferred her magic to Sela, the latter could whip up a fabulous meal with a wave of her hand, but she wanted this to be special, something she had worked at. A way of thanking Freya for everything.

Never mind that she had not quite gained control over her new powers.

Despite the times they had butted heads — okay, fought like rabid cats — recent events had cemented a friendship which both deemed invaluable.

Sela grinned to herself. *Who'd have thought her best friend would be that bat-crap crazy witch.*

A random comment, Freya had made the night all hell broke loose, popped into Sela's head. The conversation all but forgotten in the chaos that followed. It might require a quick dash into town, but it would be worth it.

Freya had fallen in love with Dublin, with Ireland — not to mention a drop-dead gorgeous bartender — where she had developed a taste for Guinness and Irish stew. Sela recalled some vague warning about the perils of the Green Fairy, but with no clue what that meant, didn't pursue it.

Sela had heard Jacob's disparaging remarks about Guinness, but this was for Freya, so Jacob could just suck it up... already knowing she would ensure there was a case of Pabst on hand.

She scoured the recipe books with no success, then turned to the internet. The image on the first link, she clicked made her mouth water, and she could almost smell the simmering dish.

Oh yes, this was an absolute must.

Shame she couldn't get the Irishman's recipe which, Freya had hinted, was a family one, passed down for generations.

She checked the cupboards and the fridge, then started a list of ingredients, the video of how to prepare the meal playing in the background.

One minute, she was twirling her pen — the next, the world around her blurred.

When it cleared, she found herself in a strange room.

Blinking it into focus, she noted the polished expanse of wood, above which hung rows of glasses and, behind, numerous bottles perched neatly along a mirrored wall.

She glanced around, cautiously. *What the actual?*

A Celtic knot with the words *The Oak Tree* was painted in gold on the sides of the bar.

A tall, bearded man with chestnut hair, a smattering of gray at the temples, and twinkling green eyes was polishing glasses.

As I live and breathe... Sean the Bartender? How is that possible?

A heady aroma teased her nostrils, and she inhaled deeply.

The man did not seem in the slightest shocked to see a stranger materialize out of thin air. He spoke to someone through the hatch behind his shoulder and, seconds later, set a steaming bowl in front of her.

Sela's mouth watered. It looked even more appetizing in real life than it had on her iPad.

Striving for nonchalance, she said chirpily, "Thank you. I'm guessing you're Sean." She arched a brow.

He grinned engagingly. "Greetings, I'm guessing you're a friend of Freya's. When you see her again, please say hello from me, and that I miss her."

Sela ate a spoonful of the stew; the rich flavour, a symphony for the taste buds.

"I am... Sela, pleased to meet you, and... wow, this is delicious. No wonder Freya still goes on about it. How are you, by the way? Sorry, she did a runner. Things got a bit messy."

"I know, lunatic deity and all that. What can you do?" He chuckled. My fault for getting involved with a goddess. I survived, had a bit o' help. Have to thank Freya for that too. I know she had a hand in it."

A dark-haired woman, obviously pregnant, appeared carrying a tray of glasses. She placed it on the end of the bar, and the smile she exchanged with Sean, left Sela in no doubt of their feelings.

She nodded at Sela and went back into the kitchen — seemingly unsurprised at the strange red-head, eating stew.

"Tara," Sean clarified. "Freya will know." He winked at Sela who smiled wryly.

"Happy to tell her everything... *if* you return the favor by giving me the recipe for this incredible stew..." Thinking, *I'm here in Dublin, it's gotta be worth the try.*

An odd shimmer prompted Sela to grab the closest solid object. Opening her eyes, she was back in the familiar kitchen. She shook her head to dispel the faint buzzing.

Did I imagine that?

Clutched in her hand, a crumpled sheet of paper.

Puzzled, she smoothed it out on the table and read the scrawled heading... *Grandma's Stew.*

Sela chuckled. "Who needs arcane alchemy when you have an Irish bartender?"

Freya's wedding would be a day to remember!

THE SELA HELSDATTER SAGA

SYNOPSES

A Flip of The Coin - Book One

What happens in Helheim never stays in Helheim.

Sela Helsdatter wishes it would. Punished for allowing her quest for power to rule her actions, she has endured eons of torment. The flip of a coin seems to offer some hope of redemption but, tasked with ridding the world of her erstwhile captor *and* lover, escape does not mean freedom.

No problem for a warrior queen... right? Wrong! Sela is no longer in ninth century Norðvegr, but twenty-first century New York with all its challenges, and where slightest misstep could spell her doom.

Aided by the most unlikely hero, Sela scours the city for her adversary, who delights in taunting her, determined to drag her back to Hell.

Will she prevail, or will A Flip of the Coin catapult her back to the abyss?

Conceived Chaos - Book Two

After ridding the world of her tormentor, and finding the love of her life, Sela Helsdatter could be forgiven for thinking she deserves a little peace.

No such luck!

Marriage to the God of Mischief is a walk in the park compared with the terror about to be unleashed from Valhalla. A diabolical edict from Odin himself sees the nine months pregnant, Sela fleeing from the entire Norse pantheon — with no clue why.

A price on her head and a target on her belly, the only person she can trust is her husband, who is keeping her in the dark. Does her unborn child hold the key to this Conceived Chaos?

Odin's Bane - Book Three

Sela Helsdatter cannot catch a break. Relentless in his jealousy and wrath, Odin is determined that neither Sela nor her infant daughter will survive.

Shattered by loss, and with no time to grieve, Sela has to rely on the one person she believes responsible for her current predicament.

A lost friendship revived, the disparate trio seek refuge in a remote corner of Montana, with the uneasy awareness the child may be the key to their salvation.

Vowing Odin will not harm a hair on her daughter's

head, Sela has to use every trick at her disposal to thwart the Norse Deity. At the same time another fiendish subversion threatens the future of humanity.

A hunting trip sparks a chain of events, culminating in a confrontation in a cave at the centre of the world.

Will Odin be victorious... or is another power stirring which will prove to be his bane?

RORI BLEU

With a smattering of riverboat pirates and royalty in her heritage, Rori Bleu's childhood reflected her past.
An interest in fairy tales, myth and legend were as important as spirited discussions around politics and current affairs — although some might argue they are one and the same!

A fascination, sparked by listening to Grimm's Fairy Tales at her grandmother's knee, not only encouraged Rori's passion for reading, but also steered her into the world of RPG's.
What began as a fun pastime, soon evolved into the creation of fantastical worlds, but Rori never lost her love of politics going on to specialise in Governmental History and Historical Research.

Naturally this means her stories are steeped in historical accuracy and real-life intrigue. While Rori's love of a happily ever after means her preferred genre is romance, don't be surprised if you discover an occasional detour into historical fiction, thrillers, horror and fantasy.

To find more of Rori's books... click the link
https://linktr.ee/roribleu

ROSIE CHAPEL

Rosie Chapel lives in Perth, Australia with her hubby and two furkids. When not writing, she loves catching up with friends, burying herself in a book (or three), discovering the wonders of Western Australia, or — and the best — a quiet evening at home with her husband, enjoying a glass of wine and a movie.

Website: www.rosiechapel.com

Also by Rori Bleu

Pineapple Meringue

Imprisoned Hearts

Port of London

Dani's Masquerade

Black Tulips

Ajei's Destiny

Porta Aeternum

The Queen's Heart

Syn *with Matthew Forester*

Echoes and Illusions *with Rosie Chapel*

Evie's War *with Rosie Chapel*

Vindicta *with Rosie Chapel*

Corrupt Covenant *with Rosie Chapel*

The Sela Helsdatter Saga with Rosie Chapel

A Flip of The Coin - Book One

Conceived Chaos - Book Two

Odin's Bane - Book Three

Also by Rosie Chapel